## BY RICHARD BISSELL

A STRETCH ON THE RIVER

7½ CENTS

In the *Rivers of America* series

THE MONONGAHELA

# $7\frac{1}{2}$ Cents

# 7½ Cents

*by* Richard Bissell

*An Atlantic Monthly Press Book*

Little, Brown and Company · Boston

ATLANTIC–LITTLE, BROWN BOOKS
ARE PUBLISHED BY
LITTLE, BROWN AND COMPANY
IN ASSOCIATION WITH
THE ATLANTIC MONTHLY PRESS

*Published simultaneously
in Canada by McClelland and Stewart Limited*

PRINTED IN THE UNITED STATES OF AMERICA
BY THE HADDON CRAFTSMEN, SCRANTON, PA.

*For*
*Juno*

# $7\frac{1}{2}$ Cents

*"Now, folks, I'm going to take you down that long line of canvas covers!"*

— THOMAS BANCROFT ROSHEK

# 1

WHEN I WOKE UP in the morning, even before I had my eyes open, I knew I wasn't in Chicago any more. No, not in Chicago, or South Chicago either, or Gary or Hammond. These small towns smell different entirely.

Then with breakfast, across the street at the Elite

[     3     ]

Café, I had to listen to this with the coffee and elastic toast:

"Was you to the dance last night out at the Royal?" says the waitress, talking through her nose.

"I was there, was you?" says a milk truck driver likewise.

"Yeah, I was there. I never seen you though."

"Well I never seen you neither."

"That's funny, I was there."

"Well, I never seen you."

"Where was you at? I never seen you."

"Well, it's funny we never seen each other."

A couple of months before, I had gone off my nut and taken a job as superintendent of the Sleep Tite pajama plant (*Sleep Tite, the Pajama for Men of Bedroom Discrimination*) in Junction City, Iowa, a trap consisting of fifty-thousand dazed customers wondering what to do after five o'clock. Town was on the Mississippi River, at least that's what they claimed — it didn't look like the pictures of the Mississippi in our geography books when I was a kid over in Gary. It didn't look like anything much. Neither did the town, unless you were interested in curiosities.

After breakfast I walked down Main Street, looking in the windows of the chain stores, and stopping to study any stray pajamas on display in other windows; then I turned to the right and up three blocks past the wholesale grocery house and the box factory and the Reliable Mfg. Co. and the Acme Products Co., and then there I was looking across the street and up six stories at The Plant.

It was a red-brick building, such as you might see in the wholesale district in any big town, with fancy granite trim up to the third story, and a couple of polished red granite pillars flanking the main entrance; carved into the stone above the door it said:

ACTION KNEE PANTS CO.
*1906*

Action Knee Pants had gone bust in 1911 but had left its tombstone up there forever. Mr. T. J. O'Hara bought the building in 1912, created Sleep Tite, and in the next ten years he made a killing (what's called a "killing" in the garment industry isn't what they'd call a killing in the Texas hotel lobbies, but it was a killing in a small Iowa town in those days) during World War I on army and navy contracts. Mr. O'Hara was a neat little dapper guy, a Yankee, now hitting his middle sixties, wore a high collar and combed his white hair straight back in a pompadour. He still "held the reins," believe me. He had wandered out here as a drummer for a Boston shirt house, and he was tighter than the bark on a tree, so they said.

"I know how many dimes it takes to make a dollar," was one of his favorite sayings, followed up with, "and how many pennies to make a dime, too."

One of the most popular indoor sports in Junction City was speculating on just how much of the town he really owned and the probable extent of his cash assets. He was not mean, or any kind of a bastard though — had a "dry wit," as they say, and quite an eye for the ladies. He was

[     5     ]

hardheaded all right but he was nice about it. He liked to give big parties and he liked beautiful, big, long, glossy black motor cars, so the legend of his being so tight was partially at least a hoax.

"He ain't so dang niggerly as what they say," as the sweeper used to remark.

He had a sap called Mr. Myron Hasler who did all his dirty work for him. Hasler was my boss.

It was about a quarter to eight, and the girls were going up the steps and pushing in through the double doors. Once inside, instead of going straight through a second pair of double doors, which would have taken them into the main office where the clerks sat around at old chewed-up desks getting sore about their wages, instead of going straight into White Collar Heaven, the girls took a left and began the climb up a wide, splintery staircase to the factory floors above.

"Well, what kind of a shape are you in this morning?" Mabel said, when I had walked through the plant and come into the office on the third floor labeled SUPERINTENDENT. "What you been up to since last night?"

"Went to the show and saw Roy Rogers riding on a horse. Went to bed."

"This ain't much of a place after Chicago, I bet," she said. "I bet you had the times over there."

"This town's all right," I said. "What's doing?"

"Boiler blew up again. Guess Ralph has the steam fitters down there already."

"Tell me something. I'm just a new young superintendent with a pair of squeaky shoes. Why don't we buy a new boiler?"

"Oh don't worry, they'll buy a new one after this one blows out a few more times. This boiler was only just put in a few years back. Why that's practically a brand-new boiler."

"Oh now listen, when was that boiler put in?"

"That boiler was put in the day after President Harding was killed. For a boiler that's not old."

"It's no newcomer," I said. "And Harding just plain died, he wasn't killed."

"Well, somebody was killed the same day. Anyways, Mr. Hasler says the boiler is like new."

"Yeah," I said. "It only blew up four times since I took this job. I'm glad it's not worn out."

I put my coat away and shoved up the black oak roll-top and sat down. The clock showed 7:50. Outside it still wasn't Chicago.

"Ralph down there on the boiler?"

"Um. Here's your mail."

Either I attract nuts or there's more nuts around now-adays — anyway, I sure get my quota of crazy letters. If it isn't a chain letter from Little Rock, where you run into a streak of bad luck if you break the chain, it's a letter from Roy J. Sprengelmeyer with a big opportunity to acquire certificates on a perpetual-motion machine. I don't know where the hell they get my name, but I'm the most popular boy in town when it comes to unloading a three-cent stamp.

The first letter I pick up this A.M. is in a dirty envelope with fancy Spencerian penmanship and the local postmark.

*Superintendent of Factory and Personelle*

DEAR SIR:

In the game of life how you play it is the leading factor, the outcome of your success or score being merely secondary.

Due to clean living and despite a gall bladder complaint dating back to the year 1922 and under the care of leading physicians ever since but not such as to impair my productivity except as regards the unfair discriminations of unseen forces largely dictated by *prejudice,* political machines, and the increase of regimentation of individual liberties even in the greatest democracy on earth and the upheaval of the tax structure, being in spite of all capable of performing a fair days work for reasonable wages and desiring at all times to associate oneself with one of the local enterprises as a local property owner rather than to go outside as has so often been necessary in the past to earn a living wage due to the scheme of things in the local scene, and in spite of physical illness too numerous to mention (among them being gall bladder complaint, Dr. R. C. Levingston performing the major operation on February 16, 1922) being able and willing at this time to accept light factory work in clean surroundings and not accepting position involving somebody else taking all the credit and glory as well as higher salary, beg to inform you am open for an offer of employment on satisfactory terms and can guarantee satisfaction of any position requiring integrity and close attention to the im-

[ 8 ]

portance of detail bearing on any subject. Therefore would welcome opportunity to discuss my capabilities for employment in above capacities and/or as tax expert and student of economics and world scene as of today.

Sincerely yours,

RODERICK M. LANSDOWN

1498 Prairie Avenue

"Well," I said. "Any time I decide to quit and go back to the big city I've got just the man to take over here as superintendent," and I tossed the letter over to Mabel.

"Oh that old fool Joe Lansdown," she said. "He don't do a lick except to set around writing these here nutty letters for jobs. Sometimes I think he's a little touched."

"What ever gave you that idea?" I said. "He sounds like a perfectly normal guy, for this town."

"There you go. I knew you'd come out with it in the long run. So that's what you think of this town. Just what I expected."

"Well, it's not much like Chicago," I said.

"What is?" Mabel said.

Mabel was about forty-three or forty-eight or fifty-one, hard to tell — one of these big energetic girls with a big bust, a lot of hair, and good-looking legs (but also solid), and she alternated between fancy printed dresses with everything on them that a sewing machine would hold together, and tailored suits, which she wore partly because she thought they made her look like a career woman such as Colbert or Roz Russell, and partly to annoy her husband. Hubby was at one of the mills, but was laid off most of the time and spent empty afternoons at Dugan's

Tavern up on West 13th Street, trying to figure out how many cards to draw.

Mabel had the goods on every operator, every cutter, and even the elevator boy, back to the first generation, including out-of-town connections and relations "on the other side of the family."

"I see you got on your extra-special Sunday School dress," I said, throwing the rest of the mail in the wastebasket. "You expecting your boy friend Hasler to visit us this morning?"

"As a matter of fact, I'll bet he *will* be up this morning," she said. "And this dress is over a year old."

I went down to the boiler room where the chief steam fitter was making fifty dollars' worth of noise while the two helpers were smoking cigarettes and leaning against the wall, cussing the wage scale.

"I seen Buster Novak's pay check last night," says one, throwing his cigarette on the floor. "A hundred and six bucks. I got a notion to go to work up there at his place if I can get in."

"Yeh," says the senior steam fitter, "and he probly put in a hunnerd and six hours. Hand me that wrench, if it ain't no trouble to ya."

"They say they're paying a dollar ninety-three up at the packing house. That ain't hay neither," says the other helper.

"Yes, George," says the senior steam fitter, "you only had nine jobs in the last two months chasin them high wages around. Why don't you go up to the packing company? I hear they give every employee a Ford car after thirty

days' service, and 200-a-month pension after you been
there eleven months. Here, hold the wrench, if you got
the strength."

"My cousin Earl he sold his herd of beef last week for
forty-eight hundred bucks," says George.

"All clear profit, of course," says the old man. "He got
the feed for nothing and his two hired men of course they
wouldn't take no wages. Now, hold onto the wrench, boy,
hold onto it, it ain't red hot. And you, junior, I hate to
interrupt them dreams of the big money and that important cigarette-smokin job, but would you please open
that valve there? Not that one for god's sake, the other
one, want to blow this factory over to Jo Daviess County?"

"Hi Frank," I said. "What's the matter this time?"

"Why this blame burner is all wore out, that's all, and
the automatic is stuck again, and some of the flues is
leaking, aside from that everything is just grand."

"Looks to me like we could use a new boiler, burner,
and maybe a new tank. Also some new steam lines. I was
looking over the lines to the buck presses on the third
floor the other day. Looks to me like they're all ready
to go."

"This whole outfit was wore out five years ago. But
I can't seem to convince nobody here. In addition to being the world's leading authority on what's wrong in
Washington, this here Hasler is also a boiler expert. He
don't know a boiler flue from a congressman, but he can
stand right there and tell me why this here old kettle is
in A-1 shape."

"I got twenty pressers upstairs, setting there drawing

wages and waiting for steam," I said. "How soon we gonna have some steam?"

"Half an hour, if these two bankers here don't faint with exhaustion."

I went out.

"They're paying a dollar eighty-four up at the Casket Company," says one of the helpers as I was going out.

"You'd be a sensation up there," the boss said. "Maybe you could get a job as tester and just lay around in them coffins all day trying them out. But listen, you must be sick, you ain't lit a cigarette for over five minutes."

I went through the stock room, past the piled-up cases of piece goods — broadcloths and prints and rayon crepes, challis and windsor crepe, outing flannel, slubs, twills, acetates, percales — past the stock boy, who was unpacking and stacking buttons from Connecticut, and entered the elevator.

The elevator boy, who had quit school because he "wasn't getting noplace there," was sitting on a wooden machine box with SINGER printed on it, getting someplace by reading the funny paper.

"Second floor," I said. "What's the flash on Marvin Stacy, Master Sleuth?"

"Oh him and Buddy, the Boy Detective, why they got this here crook trapped in the elevator shaft. They musta nicked him a couple times already, see, he's all blood to one side of his face."

"Who's the guy they got cornered this time?"

"Why this guy, his face is all like bark off a tree, they call him Bark Face."

"Has a hell of a time with all those guys, Stacy has," I said.

"Oh, him and Buddy got this here Bark Face two months ago, this here is an old Philadelphia paper I found in an empty packing case."

"If you read up on that capture a few more times you can quit this elevator stuff and go into the detective business yourself," I said.

"I been thinking of that," he said, and stopped on second.

"Don't let Mr. Hasler catch you sitting on that box reading comics," I said, getting off the elevator.

"No fear," he said.

"I don't think he'd appreciate Bark Face," I said.

The pressers were all standing around waiting for steam; they were leaning on their white tables talking or looking out the window. That little blonde O'Rourke girl was sitting on her table with her legs crossed, putting on fingernail paint. The old ladies were giving their feet a rest, sitting on the window sills.

"Well, here we are again," the forelady, a big beefy old-timer with gray hair and bloodshot eyes, said to me. "They kick if we don't get the stuff out, and then they shut the steam off. First we got steam all over the place and no pajamas coming down the chutes and I have to send the pressers home. Then we get pajamas up to the ceiling all at once and I call in the pressers and we got no steam. And I'm in the middle gettin yammered at by both sides. They must think I'm made of steam. What do I know why we ain't got steam? I suppose I'm supposed to take care of the boiler too. Oh, my god," she added in simulated terror, holding up her arms as though warding off the lash of a bullwhip, "I'd hate to think if Mr. Hasler should walk in on this and see them pressers setting there like they was at a band picnic. And O'Rourke painting her fingers! Oh, there'd be some terrible things said! I hate to think. Oh, there'd be some blood around here!" She swept her hands around indicating where the blood would flow — all over the stacked-up pairs of pajamas, across the oil-stained maple flooring to the door, and down the staircase in a crimson flood where it would knock down Ralph Budlong, the candy-machine man, and carry him right out into the street along with his stock of Dreem-Mallow bars, zestful peanut-butter crackers, and rainbow gumdrops.

"We'll have steam in half an hour," I said. The O'Rourke girl gave me the eye.

I went back up to the office.

"What's doing?" Mabel said. She was standing by the window, looking down on the roof of the Acme Products Co., and across a lot of jumbled-up buildings, toward the hills across the river. "Have a piece of gum?" she said.

"No thanks," I said.

"What's doing on second?"

"O'Rourke is painting up her fingernails," I said, flopping down at the desk.

"I bet she is. But what about the steam?"

"I believe I'll have a piece of gum after all," I said.

The Square Head: *This general type is found most frequently among successful executives and managers.*

— ASSURING BUSINESS PROFITS

# 2

AN HOUR LATER we had plenty of steam and aside from the complete collapse of a felling machine which threw the whole line out of balance and a complaint about the fans in the pants section everything was going along pretty well. Verne, the machinist, and I threw a spare felling machine into the line and I sent our own fan out of the office up to the pants section to pacify them, and in the lull that ensued I read the Sleep Tite *Flash*, the weekly bulletin to the salesmen. We had thirty salesmen peddling the line in all the states except New York, and doing pretty good, too.

Hats off to Max Weiler for his beautiful order from Halle Bros. in Cleveland!! Max has been trying to crack this top-notch account for a long time and he finally put the deal over with a GREAT BIG BANG!! Total shipment of SLEEP TITE, the modern sleep garment for Men of Bedroom Discrimination will total $1600.00. NICE GOING, MAX! And keep hitting them hard, boy. Max says the LOVERS-ON-PARADE number put this deal across. "The buyer is very price-minded," says Max, "and whereas I gave him the full demonstration of our quality features he would not budge, he is strictly price-minded, until I came to the Lovers-On-Parade number. As usual he wanted a run of sizes in that number only but I took a big chance and told him no soap I would not sell him that number alone unless he give me an order for other numbers in the line which was sure taking a chance. We don't do business that way, I said. What we want is to build on the future. He said 'Get out your order book, Max. You been bothering me for ten years with this crummy line of yours.' That is only his way of kidding of course as he said later, 'Max you got a beautiful line of goods here, you people really have a beautiful line.' "

We'll give Halle Bros., one of America's outstanding stores, swell service on this fine order, and prompt fill-ins, too. Gee that must be a grand and glorious feelin, eh Max?

Max just wouldn't take "No" for an answer.

So go get 'em, boys. With your LOVERS-ON-PARADE number you've got exclusive ammunition for the FINEST MEN'S FURNISHINGS DEPARTMENTS IN THE U.S.A.!!!

Another humdinger of an order (*another New Account incidentally*. How many New Accounts have YOU opened up in the last month? Last six months?) comes in from Frank Gipson out in South Dakota. And what do you think this was all about? Frank says:

"Levy Bros. has been giving me the go-by ever since we lost them on account of that number where the buttons all came off in 1943. They're lined up with some eastern kike outfit in Baltimore (a lousy pajama at a price), and although Mr. Levy junior (the old man has had a stroke and is pretty well out of it) and I are good friends I just never have been able to get back in. So I figured the hell with Lovers-On-Parade — with this particular acct. I mean — I'll concentrate on the *flannelette line*. Enclosed order is small but I'm back in the store again."

We call a $250.00 order for flannelettes pretty d—— good. Are you missing any bets on your territory on flannelettes? You know, I suppose, that we make the *fullest* cut, *best* construction men's flannelette nightwear in the country.

The machinist came in with his hands full of screw drivers, and slumped into the chair by Mabel's desk.

"Remember old George Hunter use to help out in the basement here?" he said.

[    17    ]

"Sure, he married a girl from Darlington her father owns the grease works. I hear he's bad," she said.

"Bad is right. I dropped in to see him last night sence I heard he was bad. My god he can't swallow, he carries his head all over to one side. He's a pityful sight. He's sufferin terrible."

"That's the way Mr. Coots was before he went, his head all over to one side like that."

"Oh hell this is worse than him, old George's head is way over like this here," and he gave a demonstration.

I looked up to see it and then went back to the Sleep Tite *Flash*.

And that brings up what to some of you otherwise keen-minded sales ambassadors is just a forgotten aspect of the Sleep Tite line. Yes, we mean NITE SHIRTS. Do you hesitate to push this line? Well, we sold over 7000 *dozen Nite Shirts* last year and the commission pays the same as the most glamourful number in the whole bewildering array of high-style Sleep Tite . . .

The telephone rang and Mabel answered it.

"Yes, yes," she said. "All right thanks honey," and she hung up.

"Oh my god," she said straightening up the cost sheets on her desk. "He's on his way up."

"Me for the wide-open spaces," said the machinist getting up.

"How long do you think he'll last?" Mabel said.

"Who?" says the machinist, putting out his cigarette.

"George Hunter, that's who we're talkin about ain't it?"

"Oh him. Why with his head all over to one side like that I give him about a month."

"They say he owns a farm over near Mineral Point," said Mabel.

"It won't do him no good to own ten farms the shape he's in," said the machinist, and he went out.

"So he's on the way up," I said.

"Yes, Loretta tipped me off."

"Well, he's been here before. Every day of his life in fact. What's the big excitement about?"

"Oh I don't know. He just rattles the devil out of me."

Mr. Hasler came into the office in about five minutes with a handful of papers — he always carried a mitt full of papers, each piece filled with trouble for somebody.

"You don't need that light on do you?" he said to Mabel. "Costs money, that light. We got to cut, cut, cut on stuff like that. We're throwing away a thousand dollars a year in this plant just on lights burning that aren't needed."

Hasler was a tall skinny old boy, bald as an egg, with bony fingers and a hook nose, a regular character. When he looked at you, you wanted to hide behind the wastepaper basket. All of a sudden you remembered a lot of things you had left undone as well as possibly a number of things you had done that he wouldn't like at all.

"And incidentally," he said. "We're not getting the right price on fluorescent tubes. Saw that purchase order the other day you sent through. Don't ever buy anything in this local market, they'll rob you every time. Seventy-six cents is no price to pay for those tubes, you can get them in case lots for 71 cents down in St. Louis."

"I just checked on past orders with Mabel here," I said. "I just figured we had some tie-up there and I had better go along."

"Mr. Coots always bought them at the Ace Electric," Mabel said. "He always got very good service."

"Mr. Coots is dead," Hasler said. "I suppose he was getting a rake-off from Munger at Ace Electric."

"Oh my," said Mabel. "Why Mr. Coots wouldn't do a thing like that. Why all Mr. Coots thought about was The Company. He was as honest as the day is long."

"Maybe," says Hasler.

"Mr. Hasler, if you want a price on lights I've got a connection in Chicago," I said, "where I can get them as cheap as anyplace in the country. I figured in a town this size you probably made a practice to give the local firms some business."

"Never mind about the size of this town, Mr. Sorokin. This is a dog-eat-dog business, you must know that or if you don't you haven't had your eyes open very wide."

"O.K.," I said. "I'll get lights for you for under 70 cents."

"That's better," he said.

Mabel got up to go out.

"Where are you going?" Hasler said.

"Why I . . . I was going to check these prices in the payroll department."

"Sit down," he said. "I want you to be here. You can check those prices later."

Mabel sat down again.

"I understand you had a breakdown in the felling department," Hasler said. "What's the reason for that?"

"Why that was that old Union Special that broke down. It really ought to have been replaced years ago," I said. "It's way out of date. It's an obsolete machine."

"Can you fix it?" he said.

"Why yes, we've got it in the shop," I said. "But it's not economical to play with these old machines."

"All right then," he said. "Fix it."

"We'll fix it all right," I said. "But I want to put in a recommendation right now for a new machine. I checked the serial number on that machine and it's a 1926 machine. The machine is obsolete."

"Don't you production men ever do anything except recommend new machines? All I ever hear around here is New Machine, New Machine."

"That's the way all the big plants do it. They don't keep any old machines on the floor," I said. "They figure a new machine pays off."

"That's 'the big plants,'" he said. "We'll do it our way and let 'the big plants' do it theirs."

"Now about this ice-cream concession in the lunchroom," he went on. "I understand this is operated by the union. Did you authorize that?"

"Why yes, I did. The union came to me and they said since the company didn't have any ice cream in the lunchroom would I mind if they got a service from the local distributor. They would take care of it and one of the girls would do the selling in the noon hour and the rest periods and we would not have to bother about it at all. Well, *we* don't want the bother of ordering and all of that, so I told them to go ahead."

"I suppose the freezer runs on electricity — who pays that?" he said.

"I suppose we do," I said. "But it's only a few cents a week."

"And in the meantime, we pay for the upkeep and operation of the machine while they pocket the profits *to fight us with*."

Well the old boy stopped me there. The doggone ice-cream concession was probably making them about two bucks a week, if that.

"I don't approve of it at all," Hasler said, stroking that big bald dome. "But I suppose it's too late to do anything now."

"We've always had a rule about smoking in this plant," he went on, "and I see you've been breaking it. That's inexperience, I suppose, but as long as you've changed the rule, all right, I'll join the new order of things."

He offered me a cigarette but I said no thanks, I had some, and then there was a big match fumble and after we got lit up he told us what was wrong in Washington and I sat there puffing like it was my first smoke.

". . . and I have it on good authority that what Roosevelt died of was not this heart condition at all but something far different. Friend of mine got it from a friend of his, Indianapolis man, who has his ear close to the ground in Washington. Anyway, say, did you hear Fulton Lewis last night?"

[    22    ]

"No," I said. "Matter of fact I very seldom listen to the radio unless it's a ball game."

"You ought to listen to Lewis at least. Say, has he got their number! Keen mind. One of the greatest political thinkers in the country today. We were going out last night to dinner over at Galena. 'Hurry up,' says Mr. Hasler, 'or we'll be late.' 'Then we'll be late,' I said. 'I don't budge until I've heard Fulton Lewis, and the car radio is out of order.' I wouldn't any more think of missing him than I'd think of skipping the morning shave."

After he was gone Mabel puffed out her cheeks and fell back in her chair in mock exhaustion.

"Say," she said. "Who is this Fuldon Lewis he is always talking about?"

"Oh," I said. "Him, he plays third base for the White Sox."

"And by the way," I said. "Didn't anybody here ever come right out and confess to Mr. Hasler that they had once voted something else besides the straight Republican ticket."

"Oh my god no," she said.

"Why not?" I asked. "It's a free country, isn't it?"

"No," she said. "It isn't. Anyway why make Mr. Hasler unhappy?"

"Yeah," I said. "We don't want to make him unhappy."

*"Mr. Mintz," Mr. Feldman said, "you are to be congratulated. Potash and Perlmutter have a reputation in the trade* nulli secundum, *and it is generally admitted that the goods they produce are* summa cum laude."

*"We make fall and winter goods, too," Abe explained.*

— POTASH AND PERLMUTTER

## 3

WHEN IT'S HOT in Iowa it's hotter than anyplace else, and that summer it was hot most of the time. That small-town summer heat is hotter, stickier, gooier, and twice as rough on the nervous system as metropolitan heat. Like everything else in the small town it is more tedious and depressing than the worst the big city can offer. After two days of it you lose your appetite and start living on lettuce and iced coffee, but the big heat wave goes on. It goes on all night, you can feel it coming in from the corn fields and creeping into your bedroom at 3 A.M. It goes on for days, weeks — weeks stretch into years and the sidewalks run like molten lava. The door handles are hot, the telephone poles are on fire, and the coins in your pocket burn your fingers. The golf links turn brown, the flowers shrivel and wilt — still the golden orb sizzles the helpless landscape, broils and fries it, and the hogs of Iowa lie inert beside the fences.

"Good corn weather," everybody says, surreptitiously plucking at their adhesive underwear.

JUNCTION COUNTY FARMER OVERCOME IN FIELD, says the daily paper.

Every week or so after I arrived on the scene an electrical storm would come in from Kansas accompanied by tornado effects and when the ear-splitting blast was over, the humidity would rise so high you could only gasp and gurgle for breath.

Frank Gipson, our South Dakota salesman, out with the Holiday Line, wrote in: "Too d—— hot nobody in the stores might as well go home I am not paying expenses nobody in buying mood out here too d—— hot for business 106 deg. in Yankton yesterday."

I had a nice apartment about five blocks from the plant, on a shady street under the hill, only they called the hill the "bluff." You think of Iowa as being flat as a billiard table with no cushions, but this town was on the Mississippi and the "bluffs" were so high and steep they even had a cable railway running up to the top.

I rented this three-room flat and had it fixed up very nice, a regular *Modern Home* magazine deal with all fancy slip covers and a couple of outlandish modern-style lamps, and a glass ash tray weighing eleven pounds — all very slick. Bedroom was not too big but had a good bed, which is the main thing and I used to manage to get some sleep by keeping the electric fan turned on all night; all my dreams were accompanied by that endless electric humming.

And such dreams — sewing machines running wild, Hasler's bald head and bony hands, bursting boilers and thunderbolts, Mabel standing on her head on her desk, animated comptometers, girls of every kind from Eskimos on down, more girls, more Hasler (always appearing at the wrong time), railroad trains, streetcars out of control on State Street, queer gnomes who danced on the ice-cream machine, endless baseball games (twenty-six innings and no score yet) — oh it was a swell summer in the sleeping department.

This neighborhood I was in was squashed right up under the hill — the hill was so steep it was a regular cliff only all covered with trees — and way at the top a bunch of little white houses perched on the edge. They could spit off the porch and it would land on our roof two hundred feet below. There were a lot of kids in the neighborhood and trikes and wagons on the sidewalks and usually once a week some gang would set up an orange crate and sell this awful-looking green drink for five cents. I drank plenty of it. As far as I'm concerned it's impossible to pass these kids with a pop stand. They are too embarrassed to ask you to buy one and they giggle and you have to start the transaction.

I joined the Elks and played some rummy and went to the movies and then I spent two or three evenings a week at home on mental improvement. This consisted of getting a book out of the library by Joseph Conrad or Henry James and then reading everything else except the book, wandering around the apartment in my stocking feet drinking beer, and fiddling with the electric fan and turning the radio on and off. I'd study the box scores, read all the letters in *Time,* and study those color pages in *Life* showing the insides of somebody's kidneys, anything rather than take that big improving plunge into Conrad.

What I needed was some female companionship, but as I am rather slow about these things I kept on with the Elks and the home evenings in the stocking feet.

"Listen," I said to Mabel one afternoon when we were sitting in the office during the 3-P.M. lull having a couple of cokes. "What would the management say if I was to take out one of the girls here in the plant?" I had my eye on a nice healthy-looking redhead if I could work around to it.

"What do you mean, 'take out'? You mean date one of them?"

"Yeah. What about it?"

"Why, they got to expect a young man like you to be up to them tricks. Especially a young man from Chicago.

[ 27 ]

Say, whoever this girl you got in mind I bet she's in for a ride."

"Or vice versa," I said. "But did any other superintendents here ever go out with the help?"

"Lord spare us," Mabel said, laughing and setting her coke bottle down among the eternal piles of cost sheets on her desk. "Why the last one we had here was so old and decrebid he didn't know whether the operators was male, female, or neutral. And the one before that had a wife would of put ground glass in his meat loaf if he would of only said 'Hello' to a Sleep Tite girl on the outside."

"Well then I think I'll take a chance," I said. "But I suppose there'll be some big reverberation from Mr. Hasler."

"No reason on earth for him to know anything about it."

"If there's anything that has to do with this factory, he knows about it. If he doesn't know about it by sundown he'll be all posted by the following noon period. I never saw a man with so much information in my life."

"Oh he was young once."

"Are you sure?"

"Oh he wouldn't raise no fuss over a thing like that," Mabel said. "But listen, I don't suppose you'd care for a nickel's worth of advice, but I spose you got O'Rourke in mind and if you'll care for my opinion you'll steer clear of that little piece, she'll spell trouble sure as the world. She already made a wreck of Clarence Freiberger and if you asked me she's just nothing more nor less than a . . ."

"Who said anything about O'Rourke?" I said.

"Well all right then."

It was June when I came into town on the streamliner and took over as the youngest superintendent they had ever had, and through the long sticky summer while the corn flourished and tasseled out on the wide rolling prairies west of town, I bored into my work and listened to Mabel. The workers were surprisingly unresentful of me as an outsider. I had been careful to tell Mabel, knowing it would immediately go over the plant grapevine, that I was up from the cutting room myself and an ex-member of the Associated Garment Makers.

I asked that redhead, her name was Catherine Williams but they called her Babe, for a date, but she turned me down.

"That wouldn't work out at all," she said. "Let's just skip that idea Mr. Sorokin."

So I got awfully jumpy and finally decided to solve my intimate problems by taking a week end in Chicago now and then. I knew plenty of girls on the South Side and all the way over to Michigan City and I didn't have to break any ice with them. Then I was ready to go again on Monday morning, to cope with Hasler and piece rates and quality kicks from customers in Butte or Mansfield, Ohio. ("We are returning today $\frac{5}{12}$ doz paj. lot #601 the felling is very poor also we note wrinkles around the lapel and on two garments buttonholes are ragged. Please send credit Memo and oblige.")

So the summer passed by and via Mabel I began to build up an inside case history on all the operators and cutters, the management, and what she called the "high folks" in town. The "high folks" was mostly the Watson tribe, three sons and all dipsos or nuts, and this famous daughter, "They say she runs around something terrible."

Then came September and no more kids with the orange crates on the sidewalk up by my house selling the bright-green drinks, and I tried to get another date with Catherine Williams but she said no, so I went to Chicago again and had a date with a belt-loop girl from the Acme Pants where I used to work.

And then came the Union Picnic.

One thing I noticed right away when I came to live in the small town is they are always talking about something that used to be here but isn't any more.

"Oh we use to have a baseball team. Sure we was in the Three I League. Why when I was a kid this here was a farm team for the Cleveland Indians and we use to send up some big talent right out of here, boys that made good in the big leagues. Hal Trosky come from here. Lots of 'em."

"Say when I was young we had a race track. Trotting races every other week."

"Oh there ain't nothing doing down on the Mississippi now but thirty years ago we had the finest boat club between St. Louie and St. Paul. In 1908 the rowing crew cleaned up every other crew in the West. And dances and balls and picnics! Oh they really put it on!"

One of the big places everybody talked about was Electric Park. This was an old-time amusement park like that one in Gary Cooper in *One Sunday Afternoon,* with a great huge merry-go-round and roller coaster and pavillions with tables for the lunch baskets. Practically everybody had got engaged there it seemed, on some romantic June night, with a box of crackerjack in one hand and the noise from the shooting gallery echoing up and down the summer spaces under the limp trees.

Half of it had burned down in the twenties and most of the rest had fallen down, but the pavillions were left and it was a very popular picnic spot, so that's where the Union Picnic was held. The union asked the company to chip in one half on the expenses but Hasler said he didn't see any reason why we were obligated to such an extent and cut it down to a quarter, about fifty dollars.

By the time I got there the cutters had been sampling the beer for about two hours and they were pretty well warmed up.

"Look out for Sammy Glaser," said Mabel as soon as she saw me. She was wiping off plates and helping out with the food. "He's in a terrible shape already poor boy."

This poor boy would never see fifty again, had got shot up in World War One and was saddled with an aged mother, and had gone the distance for thirty years with the bottle.

"Look at this place, it's a wreck," he said, when I went over to get a beer. All the men were around three big tubs of ice with Blatz, Old Style, Hamms, Potosi and Star swimming in them.

"It's a wreck. Typical of this god damn lousy town," he said. "Use to be a regular fairyland. Band concert every Sunday. Got a silver plate in my head from the Argonne Forest, myself. Whadda you think of this lousy dump? Nothing like a picnic. Look at old Hasler settin over there. Wouldn't say the word if he had a mouthful of it."

"How bout a beer Mr. Sorokin?" said Charlie, one of the cutters. "We got her good and cool by now."

"Thanks, Charlie," I said. "Give me a bottle of Star," (the local brand) "and this Mr. Sorokin part of it has gone about far enough. Over in Chicago they call me Sid. You know I used to push one of those Eastman machines myself."

"I object to such familiarity," said Sammy Glaser. "I enter an objection."

"Shut up, Sammy," said another one of the cutters. "Here, get Sid a beer."

Then we had a ball game and I played center field and dropped the only ball that came my way, but got a scratch hit and scored on the machinist's double and then we ate a hell of a lot of ham and beans and cole slaw and cake and ice cream and then it was time for speeches.

The union president got up and said it was a good thing to get away from the cares of everyday life and get together for an afternoon and evening of comradeship and relaxation. Then he made some funny sayings about various members that were behind in their dues (we didn't have the checkoff, of course) and said he wondered if these members realized what the wage standards in the industry had been as lately as twenty years ago and if they realized what they owed to the Associated Garment Makers. He said he wondered if all the members present realized how many battles had been won for them and their kiddies by their great organization. He said it was a far cry from the days of the Triangle Shirtwaist fire in New York in 1911, and the sweatshop conditions of the past. He said we should all remember our great Organization and our great former President in New York, who had given his very life for the American garment worker.

I took a sidelong glance or two at Hasler during all this and he was a sight, his jaw was stuck out and he was trying to get some kind of a half-way acceptable expression on his face but making a terrible job of it.

So then they called on me and I had enough beer in me to get up and give them a few remarks about cooperation, and then worked in some jokes about old times in the cutting room and my youthful years as a pattern-maker with a lot of schmaltz about old man Shapiro my first boss and the lessons I had learned from him. I gave them that line about we are one of the five biggest industries in the country and should be proud to be associated with it and then I got in some very original stuff about "pulling together," "the garment worker of today," "enlightened top management" and that old favorite "teamwork."

I got a big hand and it was Hasler's turn.

He said that we were in the most highly competitive business in the country and that 987 garment manufacturers had gone bust in the last five years and went on to say that everybody was better off in the old days when a man could get a schooner of Star beer for a nickel and that what was going on in Washington today was actually in the worst interests of the working classes. He said he knew he was out of order but that he had known them all since he and Sammy Glaser used to skip school together at the old Third

[ 33 ]

Ward School ("The hell we did," said Sammy in a loud voice that got a laugh), and they all knew his only interest was in a square deal for everybody. He quoted the Chicago *Tribune* and then he said that he was "a fighter," that they all knew he was "a fighter," and that he had grown up with them and knew they respected him for being "a fighter."

Everybody looked at their empty plates or up into the sky.

I spotted Catherine Williams, sitting with the girls from the pants section. She looked great. Something about that girl worked on me. A fascinating pair of eyes, for one thing —what they call the "mocking" type I guess. Anyway she had a little smile and every once in a while while Hasler was talking she'd look at one of the other girls and accentuate the sneer part of the smile by raising the corner of her mouth a bit. Every so often she would lift up her beer bottle and take a swig. She had a nice round forearm, she was a fine-looking girl.

". . . and all this socialistic-type thinking we have today . . ." says Hasler. He must have had a few beers.

I looked at Catherine Williams some more and wondered what was going on behind those big, gorgeous eyes. This girl wasn't beautiful, she just had everything I like all wrapped up in one wonderful package.

". . . regimentation . . ." says Hasler.

She caught me looking at her, but she didn't blush or look away like most girls would do, she just kept looking right back, with the same smile, as though she was saying, "Some wonderful buddy you've got here, you big sap."

". . . bureaucratic mollycoddles . . ." said Hasler.

*A Good Laugh will be had by all when the
Hoax becomes Apparent.*

## 4

AFTER HASLER SAT DOWN it took about ten min-
utes for the party to get going again, but it finally got up
some momentum and the beer bottles commenced to pass
around.

"The old boy he's quite a fire-eater, ain't he?" said one
of the cutters.

[    35    ]

"Yeah, jesus, he's sure got a line ain't he though," said another.

"Anybody know what he was talkin about?"

"He's agin it, that's all."

"I didn't hear him say nothin about that 7½ cents."

"You ain't going to, neither."

I worked around through the crowd, picked up another beer, talked with different people, kept aware of Catherine Williams's position in the pattern of the group, and all around us were the silent summer trees of the State of Iowa. It was early evening, still hot, no breeze came creeping over the hill to rustle the heavy leaves of the oak trees surrounding the garment workers' picnic.

Fulton Lewis time had come and gone. Mr. Hasler had made the Supreme Sacrifice, and having done his bit as a "fighter" on the firing line of his private war between the sewing machine and the adding machine, had retreated from the field.

"No, you ain't gonna hear about no 7½ cents until Jake gets him down and sets on his chest a while," said another cutter, who had a grand big lovely cigar stuck in his mouth.

Jake Rubenstein was the district representative of the union from Chicago.

Then my good old luck came around again: I got in a poker game with one of the cutters, the elevator boy, a hard-boiled old machine operator with gray stringy hair under her special party hat with glazed cherries on it, and Catherine Williams.

"Your Mr. Hasler come out with a real swell speech,

din't he though?" says Mrs. Hecht, adjusting the cherry-covered hat into a more becoming tilt.

"Never mind that, Mrs. Hecht," says the cutter. "I'll deal. Everybody ante 5 cents, please."

"Yeah that was wonderful," says the redhead looking at me. "Wonderful."

"Anybody besides me want another beer?" says the elevator boy.

"You keep on guzzling the free beer at that rate," Mrs. Hecht said, picking up her cards, "and we'll carry you home on a blind."

"I din't ast for no advice," says the elevator boy. "I just ast if anybody besides me wants another beer."

"Bring me one, Jimmy, while you're up," Catherine Williams said. "I'm a little dry after that last big oration about the suffering management."

"For god's sake forget it," said the cutter, an old bird with a white moustache. "We're playin cards and suppose to be havin a nice time. Lay off the politics for once, please, how about it?"

"Where'd you get the hair-do at, Babe?" said Mrs. Hecht to the redhead. "Is that a Toni?"

"No, I got this at the La Modern," says the girl. I was trying not to look at her too much, like going through the greenhouse and trying not to smell the flowers.

"I give my little granddaughter Marie a Toni Saturday. Say when I got through she was the cutest thing you ever seen."

The elevator boy came back and set down four beers.

"None for me," says Mrs. Hecht.

"I din't bring you none," says the elevator boy.

"What granddaughter is that — is that Claude's little girl?" Catherine Williams inspected her cards.

"That's right. She'll be three next month."

"You shouldn't ought to give a little kid that age a home permanent," said the elevator boy, sitting down again.

"What a game," said the cutter to himself. "Home permanents now."

"I heard that's not so good for their hair," said the elevator boy.

"Who from?" Mrs. Hecht said with bitter scorn. "Who was you endulging in conversation on the subjeck of home permanents with might I politely ask?"

"Why it might a been my Aunt Rose, that's who it was. She and this neighbor lady was goin over the subjeck."

"Well listen, Mister Genius," said Mrs. Hecht, "just go tell your Aunt Rose to relax, because there ain't nothing to it. Who dealt? What's the game? Tell your Aunt Rose she better ketch up with the rest of the world."

"I'll take two cards," Catherine Williams said. She had a few freckles. She still had that independent look around her mouth.

Somehow or other I managed to get her into my car, her and Mrs. Hecht, for the ride back to town. Maybe it was the beer, but she had quit fighting and sat in the middle. I felt her beside me. We dumped the old lady at her house.

I drove away like I was going away, but I just drove up the side of the street a few houses away and stopped.

I turned out the lights. She started to move away from me.

"Come here," I said.

"Speed artist," she said.

"Come here, Catherine," I said.

She slid across the crummy velours and I put my left hand around her waist and my right hand behind her head, feeling the color of her beautiful hair against my fingers, and I kissed her cheek right where I'd been wanting to all evening, and all I could say, could whisper in her ear, was "Baby!" Eloquent bastard I am.

So then I kissed her and the angels gathered on the sidewalk beside us and sang songs and played on their mouth organs.

We didn't say a goddam word for twenty minutes, a record for me at least. All that time we were kissing, and when I put my hand on her breast, instead of pulling my hand away in the usual stupid manner, she put her hand over mine, as light as could be.

To tell the truth she tasted of beer, not like milk and honey, but I kept whirling and whirling down and down, then up and up on the waves of kissing and kissing, while she held her hand on mine.

"Gee," I said finally. "Gosh you're terrific, baby."

"You're not so bad yourself," she said. "For a superintendent."

*We start getting some cold nights out here on
the plains pretty soon so how about getting the
flannelette paj. out to the trade on time for
once?*

— FROM THE TERRITORY

# 5

"THAT WAS SOME PICNIC," I said. "I never
thought it was going to end up like this."

"Let's get out of here," she said.

"Listen," I said, "it's still early, let's you and me stop
off in some gin mill and have a drink. I've had enough
beer to last me until next year. How about it?"

[    40    ]

"O.K.," she said.

"I like this town a hell of a lot better than I did an hour ago," I said.

"Let's go," she said.

"Give me another smooch," I said.

"Mmm," she said.

We went into the first place where there was a beer sign and it was some trap. In back they were playing cards. All you could smell was beer and cigar smoke and the lavatory and the dusty paper roses behind the bar.

"Good evening folks," said the bartender pausing to spit.

"Got any whiskey?" I said. Whiskey is against the law in taverns in Iowa.

"I got Sunnybrook or Kinsey Gold," he said, sticking his finger in his ear.

"Sunnybrook and a coke," I said. "What d' you want, Babe?"

"That's O.K.," she said.

"Make it two," I said.

He reached down and opened a cupboard and got out the whiskey.

"You know you don't seem like a small-town girl to me," I said. "You seem different somehow from the other girls I see around town."

"This is the greatest snow job since the blizzard in 1938," she said.

"What do you do with yourself, anyway? You have fun here?"

"Oh I go out with rich millionaires and to parties up at Watsons' house on the hill."

[    41    ]

"Watson Since 1872," I said. "Watson, a Pump for Every Purpose."

"That's the idea. Gee, this is some wonderful night club we are in."

"We'll do better next time," I said. "Where do all your boy friends take you?"

"Across to East Junction is supposed to be the big thrill around here. I don't go out very much though."

"With a face and a shape like that! Why not?"

"Calm down now, don't get excited," she said. "I'm terrific, it's true, but don't overdo it."

"Why don't you go out more?"

"If you must know I don't go for the local romeos. They put on a loud necktie and they think they are all dressed up. Then they take you to a floor show of midgets or trained dogs or girl cornet players and they buy you a burnt steak and some punk highballs and they figure you should give them everything except your shoes."

We stood it for a couple of drinks more in there and then I took her home.

Her house was on a hill looking down over the Milwaukee railroad yards, a little white house where she lived with her old man who was a conductor on those seventy-five car freight trains.

"My Dad is off on his run," she said. "So you can't come in."

"That sounds like a damn fine reason for coming in," I said. "Let's make some coffee for example. How about it?"

"No dice. It so happens we've got neighbors, lover, who

have spent the last ten years trying to get some dirt on Babe, so we'll just sit right here for a while and then you can run along home to your little bed."

"Listen, when are we going out again?" I said. "Some night when we don't have to play poker with Mrs. Hecht and listen to Hasler. I'll buy you a burnt steak and a bunch of punk highballs and we'll have a hell of a time. Maybe we can find a floor show where they toss Indian clubs."

"You're crazy," she said when I had quit kissing her. "Hasler would blow his stack if he heard you were going out with one of the famous Sleep Tite girls."

"The hell with him," I said. "I'm lonesome, honey. I'm all alone over here — I been hanging around the Elks Club and all that but this is the first time I've had any fun in two months."

"Listen, tell me something," she said. "How old are you, anyway?"

"I'm twenty-eight," I said. "And I know how old you are because I looked it up on your employment card."

"Oh, *honestly*," she said.

"You're twenty years old and your telephone number is 4926. You're female, white, have one parent living and your address is 1918 Railroad Avenue North."

"You know I didn't like you at all at first," she said.

"Uh huh," I said.

"I didn't think I would like you very much," she said. "I thought you were terrible. I thought you were stuck-up and conceited. You look like an awful sap down at the plant."

"You've got green eyes, too," I said. "Remember when

[    43    ]

you looked at me while Hasler was giving his speech?"

"What about it?"

"Nothing. It was nice. You looked at me like you thought I was a dope."

"That's what I thought."

"What do you think now?"

"Well, you're a big-city dope instead of a small-town dope, anyway. That makes a difference."

"Let's go in the house."

"No," she said.

So we kissed for about ten minutes and I got my hand inside her dress and investigated those, and a freight train entered the north end of the yard and worked down through the yard chuffing slowly. I could smell the soft coal smoke mixed with Babe's perfume.

"You know my telephone number and everything," she said. "That's a joke."

"I picked you out the first day I walked through the plant," I said. "I saw you there setting sleeves a mile a minute and I said, 'There's a small-town dope worth investigating.'"

That was a big lie, I hadn't even noticed her for over a month, or any other girls either, the first month.

"Oh what a big lie," she said. "You didn't even know I was alive until after you'd been here over a month. Not until some time in August."

"How do you know so much?" I said.

"Never mind, I know when you started looking at me in that foolish way down at the plant. Honestly you are a scream down there. Oh men are so funny, especially you."

"Babe, let's go in the house," I said.

"No," she said. "Listen, if you want me to take the bra off, O.K., but you'll never get it off with one hand like that yourself. Here, quit that silly fumbling around and let me do it."

"O.K.," I said. "You do it. I'm just a dumb man."

"There now," she said. "Aren't they nice?"

"Listen, maybe I'm funny," I said. "But you're the funniest I ever met."

After a long time she said she had to go. So we had six false departures and farewells and some more kissing and giggling and sighs and more smooches.

"You know I worry about you," she said. "You seem so nice and innocent. . . ."

"And conceited and foolish," I said.

"And conceited and foolish, and you poor boy you're in for a lovely big pile of trouble down at the plant. You're in for a hell of a time, darling dope."

"What the hell are you talking about?" I said. "What kind of trouble?"

"I'm talking about the contract, lover," she said. "Seven and a half cents worth of trouble."

Nice way to end the evening.

But I didn't give a damn anyway.

*Mr. Updegraff (listlessly) — What are you going to do with that old sewing machine back there — open a sweatshop?*

— S. J. PERELMAN

# 6

THE NEXT DAY was a beautiful day. Maybe it was raining, I don't remember, but it was a beautiful day anyway. All I had to do was think about last night and I felt good.

I came in the plant and rode up in the elevator.

"They say he's a solid mast of cancer," the elevator boy said to the fourth-floor forelady.

[    46    ]

"I don't know about him," she said, "but I know his nephew over to Cuba City died of tumors. The lumps turned all black and blue."

"Did he suffer?" says the elevator boy.

"Let me off on three," I said.

"All over black and blue tumor lumps? What do *you* think?"

I strolled through the third floor among the Singers and Union Specials and said Good Morning, Good Morning, and stopped to talk with the forelady for a few minutes about the girl who wanted to quit and the new buttonhole machine and the feud in the pants-felling section; and I listened to the daily complaint about the rotten cutting and she said, "Sometimes I just wonder why I don't move on. I could keep house for my brother out in South Dakota. He's after me all the time," and she gave a big resigned sigh, "I can't seem to please nobody. I try to do my best but I guess it ain't good enough. My brother says . . ."

"Listen," I said. "You're doing fine. It wouldn't be the garment business if we didn't have trouble all day long. You wouldn't like it out in South Dakota."

"My brother he's a parish priest out there and he says . . ."

I went in the office and opened my mail and looked over the Cutting Report and the Production Report and the parts invoices and a note from the Time-Study man saying that hell was about to bust loose on the collar-setting job any minute, and Mabel never said a word.

"Well," she finally said, hammering away on the comptometer. "How'd you get along with your new lady friend?"

"We drove over to Freeport and got the Justice of the Peace up and got married," I said. "We're expecting twins."

"Ooooh, listen how mad he gets. Must be serious."

"Yeah," I said. "It's a terrific love affair that will probly bust Eastern Iowa wide open."

"Look out," she said. "Here he comes. I can tell his footsteps."

Hasler came in and sat down with a handful of papers.

"Your talk was all right," he said. "But I hope you're not too easy. This is a fight to the finish whether you know it or not. They're out to take us over. They're out to get this plant, lock, stock, and barrel and we've got to fight. They're clever, they're shrewd, you got to be a student of it, bore in behind the scenes to know what's going on. Don't give an inch, my boy. Keep your fists up."

I didn't know what to say so I said nothing.

"It was a lovely picnic," Mabel said. "Everybody had a grand time."

"We never had picnics when I started in this business," Hasler said. "Worked till eight and nine o'clock on Friday nights and no overtime. All this picnic stuff is a lot of fol de rol. New Deal socialistic nonsense."

Hasler's hands exerted a morbid fascination over me. I hated them but kept looking at them anyway. They were big and white, and he had long "spatulate" fingers. I can't stand huge hands. And especially big thick flat fingers.

"Do you belong to the Associated Foremen?" he said.

"Why no," I said. "I was a foreman in Gary for about a year but they didn't have it over there."

"Well, we'll pay your membership. There's a meeting Thursday. I'll send your ticket and membership card over to you. We've got a fine speaker this week. Think his topic is 'Be a Builder,' something like that."

"But I'm not a foreman," I said. "They probably won't feel too happy to see me at their meeting, not to mention the way I'll feel."

"My god, boy, *I'll* be there. Why everybody in top management will be there."

"I don't get it," I said. "What's it all about? I thought you said it was a foremen's club."

"Boy, some of these foremen are all crazy on this socialistic stuff and they want a union. So management has got up this Associated Foremen to have meetings and speakers to show them they're part of top management and get 'em over this union idea. We have a chummy get-together and some fellowship and usually a good speaker and make them feel they are on the Management Team. It's a big movement."

"It sounds big," I said. "How do the foremen like it?"

"By and large they are keen on it. Some of the radical element of course are spreading out a lot of rotten propaganda against it, but all in all the movement is going ahead very fine." He waved the papers bunched up in his hand. He was always gesturing and pounding a fist into an open palm or stabbing a finger at you like an advertisement command from the Burton Mail Technical School in Kansas City to MAKE MORE MONEY IN AIR CONDITIONING!

"I hear they had an awful time up at the canning factory with some of the foremen. They just flatly refused to join," said Mabel innocently.

"There's some rotten apples in every barrel," Hasler said. "You never know where these Communists'll turn up nowadays."

Enter hurriedly from left, the machinist, with a handful of screw drivers.

"Oh, well, I suppose you're busy," he said to me. "I'll see you later."

"How are you this morning, Verne?" said Hasler with determined good fellowship. "Didn't drink too much beer I hope."

"Oh, I'm about the same," Verne replied, slumping against the door jamb. "Only my ole kidney trouble seems to be flarin up again. Then I been havin these here terrible headaches lately. I went to that new chiropractor up on 13th Street, has his office right over the Karmel Krisp Shop, you know where I mean? He says to me, 'I don't want your money,' he says, 'unless I cure you. I ain't going to accept a red cent on any other basis other than a complete and irrevocal cure of your ailment and condition,' he says. 'That's fair enough,' I says. 'Go to it Doc.' "

"Waste of money, my boy," Hasler said. "I strongly advise . . ."

"How's he doin?" Mabel asked.

"Oh hell, he's thumpin along at a great rate," said the machinist. "I don't notice no change yet, though. These here kidneys of mine . . ."

"Did you give him any money yet?" Mabel asked. "I'll bet he pried some money loose in spite of the fancy talk."

"I give him ten dollars so far."

"I knew it," Mabel said, getting up and going to fiddle with the venetian blinds. Give a woman a venetian blind to play with any day. Mabel could give those old slats plenty of exercise, especially in moments of excitement or triumph. "Oh they're wise those fellows. They can smell out a dollar bill, I tell you."

"Verne, give a look at that high-speed Reece machine will you?" I said.

"Right! chief," he said and disappeared.

" 'Right! chief,' " said Mabel. "He must of heard that in the movies. Him and his kidneys."

"How are sales, Mr. Hasler?" I said. "Can we count on steady work for a few months now?"

"Slow. Very slow. Business is just dragging."

"That's what I wanted to know. Maybe I better lay off some of the newer help before the work runs out."

"No, no, don't do that," he said. "Orders are holding up fairly well. We'll have work. Keep 'em on the job. We got to make deliveries."

O'Rourke came into the office. She held out a finger to Mabel.

"What's the matter honey?" Mabel said.

"Just burnt my finger on that ole flatiron of mine. It ain't bad. Just put a piece of tape on it for me will ya honey?" O'Rourke said in her baby-doll, squeaky voice. She had an upswept hairdo and a lot of make-up and a 37½ inch bust measure.

"Better check that with the doctor, young lady," said Hasler. "Can't be too careful with a thing like that."

[     51     ]

"Just gimme a pieca tape," she said, not paying any attention to Hasler. He was paying plenty of attention to her, on the other hand.

"How did this accident happen?" Hasler says, all solicitude and determined to get in the act.

"Why O'Rourke here just burnt her finger on her iron that's all — that happens every once in a while."

"And as I was saying, business is very poor," Hasler said, for the benefit of O'Rourke. He figured she'd take that right back out to the plant. "Orders are not holding up at all. Competition is tougher every day."

"Too bad how some people suffer, ain't it?" O'Rourke squeaked to Mabel. "Thanks for the Band-Aid honey," and she went out, wiggling her ass in three-quarter time.

Hasler turned red. He got it. Didn't look so smart sometimes but he got that one.

"What's her name?" he said.

"That's O'Rourke," Mabel said.

"Better keep an eye on her," he said.

"Everybody in town, especially the men, have had an eye on her for ten years, since she was fifteen," Mabel said. "That won't be hard."

"I think *you* know what I mean, Sidney," Hasler said.

He was playing the good fellowship mighty strong on this famous September morning after the night I took Babe Williams home. He'd never called me by my first name before.

The machinist reappeared. When Hasler was in the office he just couldn't stay away for fear he'd miss something he could tell over the spareribs and kraut at supper.

"I checked that Reece," he said. "Oh, excuse me, I guess you're busy."

"Think I better have the factory man over to give it an overhaul?" I said.

"No, I found out the trouble," he said. "I got her going O.K. again. She ain't going to break no more threads for a while."

"Business," says Hasler to me. "You were asking me about business. Well, it's very erratic. The dealers have apparently got a big inventory and since the war and all nobody seems to be buying pajamas. Learned to sleep in their 'BVDs' during the war years in the armed services all these young men did. Doubt if they'll ever buy pajamas now. We've got to play the female angle. Lovers-On-Parade number is a help, but trade is slow, very slow."

On my desk was the Sleep Tite *Flash*.

Harry Bodenheim has just landed the sweetest account in the whole state of Oregon [it said]. He sold the Black & White Stores, a twenty-seven store chain, their entire Holiday requirements. Across the glorious U.S.A. in old New England Louis Marchand clinched Filene's for a total of $2900 and old Beantown will be resplendent during the Yuletide season with gifts galore of Sleep Tite high-style pajamas for men with Romance, men who *care* about their Bedtime Appearance. It's the same from coast to coast, orders are pouring into your Sleep Tite headquarters like never before. Sales are topping all highs in your industry. Records are falling into the discard with every Monday mail. Frankly we thought last year was good. It *was* good. It was stupendous. *But this year is* BETTER. *Are* YOU *cashing in?*

[     53     ]

"Our costs are eating us alive," Hasler said. "We're not making a dime. Just trading dollars. We've got to throw out half the Sales Force. Dead wood has to go. Competition and high factory costs are killing us. The Administration in Washington has destroyed . . ."

Off the Record [said the mimeographed Sleep Tite *Flash* in front of me with a rubber stamp pad holding it down] pajama business is running 18 per cent ahead of last year. Are YOU . . .

"Verne," I said, "do me a favor and check Rosenmeier's 51400 seamer will you? She's got some beef or other."

"Right! chief," said Mabel sotto voce.

"Right! chief," said Verne, departing.

"Mr. Hasler," I said, "I've got some bad news I picked up last night at the picnic. Might be nothing in it but anyway — well, maybe you've been approached already."

"What's this? What're you talking about?" he said. He rubbed his nose and looked intense. He knew all right. And I knew that he knew that I knew it.

"They want an increase," I said. "They want 7½ cents."

"I want a steam yacht and a colored boy in a monkey jacket to bring me highballs on a silver tray," he said instantly.

"Looks like neither one of us is going to get what he wants," he said.

*"Well, the jolly old guerre est finie. What now?"*

*"Let's get back on the —— in' job, youse, this don't change nuthin'."*

– F. R. LACY IN CONVERSATION (16 August, 1946)

# 7

BABE AND I would go to the movies and see the movie queens in their make-up, some with hair that seemed to be made of neoprene or spun rayon. We underwent the Donald Duck torture, and wondered what ever happened to the two-reel comedies with people in them. Bogart said, "Listen, get this straight, you two-bit muggs," and Jimmy

[ 55 ]

Stewart said, "We-ll now, I don't know about that," and Betty Hutton screamed and others tap danced, punched each other, shot pistols, crashed planes or said, "You made me learn to Care." Then we would drive around, up and down the tedious hills or perhaps out the highway a few miles west to see the cornfields in the moonlight (a very dull sight compared to the steel mills at night). I was trying to get her to come up to my joint but she was not in favor of that so all the romance was taking place in the car, which is no good at all but better than nothing. The goddamn squad car is always showing up at the wrong time with its spotlight and anyway it is uncomfortable and you are always getting a cramp or somebody's leg goes to sleep; when it is all over instead of being someplace you have to start the car and go away to some other place, home or Hamburger Heaven or up Main Street.

Well I figured all this has got to end we are big kids now and let's cut out the high-school stuff and get organized here.

So it got to be an evening in late September and we piled in the heap as usual and drove over the bridge to Illinois.

"Saddest excuse for a river I ever saw," I said. "The mighty Mississippi!"

"You oughtta see it from the deck of an excursion boat, like the *Capitol*, on a moonlight excursion," Babe said. "Then you'd see what it's all about. They have this great big dance floor . . ."

"Beer, drunk farmers . . ." I said.

"You can look over the back end and see the paddle wheel," she said.

"Blown lunches, cheap cigars," I said.

"They start playing the calliope about an hour before the boat leaves. You can hear it way up on the hill. Takes me back to when I was a kid," says Babe.

Across the river in East Junction the license plates on the cars are mixed about evenly: Illinois, Iowa, Wisconsin. Then there's always a few cars from Minnesota, Missouri and Indiana, and some Model A's with the back end cut out with a torch and made into pickups and these have so much mud on the plates you can't tell.

The street is a wide old western street and is the only street in town and down both sides there is a competition among the tavern keepers to see who can put up the flashiest electric sign. There are eighteen saloons on one side and fourteen on the other, and the neon salesmen have done a wonderful job with their sales quotas — the place makes Broadway and 42nd Street look like Monday night eight miles west of Topeka.

"Don't, you'll ruin my make-up," says the Babe.

So then we went into the Sixty-Six.

"And now folks, it's our pleasure to welcome you once again to the Club Sixty-Six, where you can always be sure of the latest in satisfaction of both Food and Fun," squawks the genial M.C. as Babe and I order a drink while sitting at a ringside table. "So relax, have fun, and forget the cares of the day at the Club Sixty-Six, always something doing and drinks and food the way *You* like to have them prepared. So let's call upon Ray and his staff of trained mixologists for the latest in tempting beverages while we enjoy another stellar attraction in entertainment brought to you

[    57    ]

direct from Hollywood, California. Folks, let's meet and greet none other than Stan Marco in 'Foibles and Fantasies.'"

"I'll bet he's got Indian clubs," I said.

"Shut up," Babe said. "Give the boy a break."

"Stan!" says the M.C. in comic bewilderment. "Come out here kid."

Nobody showed up.

"And now folks," says the M.C. into the mike again, "let's meet and greet none other than Stan Marco in his clever production entitled 'Foibles and Fantasies.'"

The orchestra (drum, sax, electric guitar and Hammond organ) gave an entree, heavy on the drums.

Nobody appeared.

Well, to make a long story short Stan Marco was found behind the bass drum asleep and after being poked and prodded he got up and tottered out very sleepy to the mike. He pulled a half-eaten ham sandwich out of his pocket and took a bite.

"For Christ sake," I said. "That's Stan Marcowitz from Gary. I went to school with him. Craziest bastard in town."

"You mean you know him?" said Babe.

"I'm tellin you baby I went to high school with him. His brother Ike was All-Indiana High School first team. Stan fell off the roof of the shed back of Cohen's Drug Store and broke his arm when we was in sixth grade. His sister's name is Rose. Used to go around with my sister Ruth." I dumped my highball down the hatch.

Stan was fiddling with the mike like all the entertainers do and was about to give his impression of Eddie Cantor.

[    58    ]

He was working hard. The crowd was going along with him, but they weren't giving much yet.

"I suppose you use to go out with his sister, too," Babe said.

"No but she was some looker," I said. "She married some guy from Niles, Michigan. Some big operator over there."

"Must be a lot of big operators in Niles," she said. "It's such a big place."

"Big enough, Miss America," I said. "Big enough."

Stan spotted me and came over after the act and sat with us so instead of us getting out into the fresh air of Main Street at ten o'clock and comparatively sober, we stayed for another show and didn't get out until after one A.M. and well loaded at that. It took a couple dozen of those pale one-ounce highballs to put it over, but if you have the fighting determination and enough one dollar bills you can eventually feel that mystic glow on Club Sixty-Six highballs.

Stan and the girl and I sat and threw them down from ten until one A.M. and hashed over all our troubles and triumphs and went into the modern history of everybody in Gary which must have been very interesting to the redhead.

"And Harry Kosciuszko, the mad genius of East Chicago, where is he at, Sid?"

"Harry's still at the Art Institute," I said. "I think he's got a permanent home there. Anyway he's going into his tenth year as an art student."

"What the hell does he do besides take out them models and all?" Stan says.

"Why damn it you ignorant shlemiel," I said. "He paints

pictures. He sure ain't there to learn bookkeeping or the piano accordion."

"Sounds fishy as hell to me," says Stan. "If you ask me he's nuts."

"Who ain't?" I says. "Look at the thing like this: Your old pal Sidney Sorokin who was going to set the world on fire is superintendent of a garment plant in a two-bit town in a place called Iowa; you're chasing around the country spending your evenings giving the yokels your impressions of Eddie Cantor, and Harry is a ten-year art student with a baggy tweed suit. So who is the most nuts?"

"Well, we ain't none of us tellers in a bank anyways like brother Ike," says Stan. "Sid, you oughtta see the All-Indiana fullback behind the bars at the Third National Bank and Mistrust Co. It's a sight, kid."

"Why that's what I'm tryin to get across to you," I said. "Would you rather Harry was counting the bank notes into packages and slipping rubber bands on? You think he'd look good in a little gray coat selling cigarette lighters at the United Cigar Store? Quit kickin about Harry, you and your impressions of Eddie Cantor for christ sake."

"Aw I'm just developin myself on these jobs. Just keep your eye on me, I'll be up there," Stan said, signaling Louis for more hooch.

"Well I got a startling piece of news for you, sweetheart," I said. "Harry's gonna be up there too. You look at his pictures, you can't see nothing hardly. Looks tough. Looks like poor old Kosciuszko the madman of East Chicago is wasting his time. 'What the hell is it all about?' you say. All you can see is queer arrangements of colors and disembodied people floating around. Then maybe in another one he's got this strange horrible-looking mottled bottle green background with a hand, all wrinkles, in the foreground, with big fancy rings on the bony old fingers. What's the title? 'Springtime In Peoria.' Sounds like the boy has gone off his rocker, don't it?"

"All them artists are nuts," Stan said.

"Well, I met a girl last summer was also a student at the Art Institute. 'Did you ever hear of a guy named Harry Kosciuszko?' I asked her. 'Good-looking guy with . . .'"

"Whadda ya mean 'good lookin?'" says Stan.

"'A good-looking guy with a scar on his cheek? Real dark eyes? Talks a mile a minute?' 'Oh,' she says, 'everybody knows Kosciuszko. He won Second Prize in the All-Chicago show last year. He's a genius, they say.' 'He wasn't when I knew him,' I says. 'He just had the title. He musta grown into it.' 'He's terrific,' says the doll. 'He uses a completely unique palette. His imaginative effects are amazing.' Or 'superb' or 'devastating' or something."

"I wonder if there's any money in it," Stan says. "I bet he don't clear fifty a week with that unique mallet of his."

"Would Harry care? You know him."

"I guess he wouldn't, no I'll admit that crazy bastard wouldn't. But by god I care. You think I'm enjoyin this Eddie Cantor routine, this here jumpin around from one rube town to another? Playin those lousy dates around Chicago where the customers are all so loaded they can't even see the floor? Settin around waitin to do the next show? Eddie Cantor! Listen boy I've got a Noel Coward routine that is solid class. I used it last winter in Detroit. *Variety* caught the show and give it a big rave. 'Marco's relaxed style and clever presentation rang the bell at this plushery,' it says in *Variety*. 'Boy shows flashes of real talent. Got good mitt.' Well, that's all swell but can I use that stuff here? Who the hell in this bunch of hon-yocks ever heard of Noel Coward?"

"Not me, I'll guarantee that," I said.

"He's that English guy that was in *Human Bondage*," says Babe. "With a bum leg or something. Let Bette Davis walk all over him and make a big sap outa him."

"No, no, honey, that was Leslie Howard," says Stan. "Coward is strictly high class. Legit stuff. But what about you, Sid, how you makin out? Big superintendent now, hey?"

"Yeah, very big superintendent," says Babe. "They don't come any bigger."

"But tell me kid," Stan said. "How do you make it here in a jerk town like this on a permanent basis? I mean after Gary and Chicago and all? Don't it get a little boresome?"

"It was," I said, "very boresome until I met up with the redhead here."

"Yeah, that could change a lotta things," Stan said, looking at Babe and giving her that crazy crooked Polish smile of his.

"Let me give it to you straight, Stanley," I said, "so you won't think I'm off my nut like Kosciuszko. I got everything planned out years ahead, boy. I'm like you, kid, I want to get my hooks into some of that nice money. My old man, and yours, too, and Harry's, they all knocked themselves off on them open hearths. Not for me. Listen, boy, there's no money for the hired help in the manufacturing end of the garment setup. I know that. Like you say, 'I'm developin myself on these jobs.' Pretty soon I'm gonna know every last inside trick of the manufacturing end. Then you know what I'm gonna do?"

"You tell me, russki, then what you gonna do?"

"Then I'm gonna move over into management. I got a Noel Coward routine of my own, Mr. Marcowitz. Right now I'm on the Eddie Cantor imitations out in the sticks, but just be patient, old pal, and you'll see me in the Empire Room on State Street, entertaining the big customers and eating three pound lobsters. Me and Ralph Ginsburgh and his violin are gonna be as thick as thieves."

"You and Ralph Ginsburgh will make a lovely couple," says Stan. "In the meantime, you never answered my question. How the hell do you stand it over here? And how do you get along over at the plant with the yokes?"

"Oh I got no troubles at the plant," I said. "I got about sixty obsolete machines they won't replace, and a boss with a sunny disposition like Adolf Hitler, and a strike about to explode under my feet any day now — why everything is as peaceful as Sunday afternoon out in the Michigan dunes."

"I don't want you boys to think that I'm a rotten egg or anything," said Babe, "but I gotta go home. It's instructive and all that listening to you boys but I gotta clean house tomorrow."

"If you need any help with the vacuum cleaner call me up," said Stan. "But listen, only ten minutes till the next show. Stick around. For you I'll do the Noel Coward routine, even in East Junction."

"Stan, boy, we gotta go," I said. "We'll catch you next year at the Latin Quarter. We gotta get outa here and on the trail."

"Yeah, I spose so," he said. "Well, been quite a reunion ain't it? I hope we didn't bore you with all this talk about old times in Greater Chicagoland," he said to Babe. "You see honey, all us slavs like me and Harry Kosciuszko and your boy Sid here, we're all tryin to be a credit to our poor old parents, which they all come over for us kids to be a big success in the Land of Opportunity. You got a good boy here," he says. He's kind of a silly old bastard but over in Gary Indiana he is hot rocks."

"You're loaded," I said.

"True, true," he said.

"Good-by," the redhead said. "We'll see you again. I want to see that Noel Coward stuff sometime."

"Yeah. O.K.," he said. "So long. I'll see you kids around. Better move to Chicago before you go crazy over here."

Outside the cold early fall air with a little smoke in it from grass fires along the bluffs by the river mingled with the smell of French-fried potatoes blowing above the lime-stone sidewalks. I held onto the girl's arm and we went around the corner and she slid in her side of the car and I walked around and got in my side and stuck the key in the ignition. But I didn't turn it on, instead I reached for Miss Williams and we fell into a long deferred embrace. With my eyes closed I could feel the whole Middle West from Fort Wayne to Omaha, all around us. Right up against me I could feel Babe Williams.

"Let's go home," I said. "This thing has gone far enough. I'm tired of this wrassling in the car."

"Gimme a cigarette," she said.

"You smoke too much, baby," I said.

"Gimme a cigarette," she said.

We went across that big steel bridge from Illinois over the mighty Mississippi into the state of Iowa, and gave the man at the toll gate 20 cents and a fond farewell.

"I'm not going up to your place," she said.

"The hell you're not," I said. "We're all grown up now, we're big kids," and I turned north up the street that ran under the hills toward "my place." In the sky over the frame houses of the South End burned a blazing signal: HOTEL HAWKEYE. The "downtown" district was built on the flood plain of the Mississippi and wherever you were at night you could look up and see HOTEL HAWKEYE in the sky. Then to the west, hanging in the night right over the town, were the lights of houses on the edge of the bluff that rose beside the town. Like Pittsburg.

"Somebody will see us go in," she said.

"No they won't," I said. "Nobody will see us go in. Where's your Dad tonight?"

"He's at the other end. He's in La Crosse," she said. "He'll be down on number 78 at 9 A.M. tomorrow."

"Nobody will see us go in," I said.

"I bet they will," she said.

"No they won't," I said.

*Never shall I be able to understand that two
women aren't better than one, three better
than two, and ten better than three.*

— GUY DE MAUPASSANT

# 8

I TURNED ON THE LIGHTS in my joint and kissed
Babe.

"That's modern art, I suppose," she said, looking over my
shoulder.

"Yeah, that's one of Harry Kosciuszko's pictures," I said.
"The guy Stan and I were talking about."

"Say, he's pretty good," she said. "I like that. It's goofy as hell but it's kinda nice."

"Yeah, so am I," I said. "But listen sweetheart, we didn't come up here to talk about Kosciuszko."

"Didn't we?" she said. "What did we come up here for?"

"For god's sake don't get going like that," I said. "I'm nuts about you, Babe, let's not have a lotta jokes right now. If you don't wanna do it tell me right now and I'll take you home. I couldn't stand two hours talking about modern art and whether the Yankees are gonna cop the series or not."

"We'll get around to you after I look your place over," she said giving me her coat. "Gee, Sid, you've got it *nice* here. Who fixed it all up like this anyway?"

"*I* did for god's sake. What'd you think I lived in, a cold-water flat with a folding cot and a couple army blankets?" I said, hanging up her coat. "Damn," I said, trying to find a coat hanger and knocking down a couple of my coats.

"What's the matter now?" she said, turning on the radio.

"Nothing," I said. "But I wish I could some day hang up something in a coat closet without everything else falling down."

"You're nervous," she said. "Gee I thought you were a big sophisticated boy from Chicago."

"I'm not nervous," I said. The hell I wasn't. On a deal like this I'm real sensitive. I want everything to go just right. I think about it a lot and when it happens I get nervous like I was going to my first dance.

[     67     ]

"What's your friend call it?" she said.

"Call what?" I said, dumping a couple ash trays into the wastebasket and pulling the shades down.

"That picture," she said.

"He calls it 'The Temptation of Indiana Harbor,'" I said.

"What's that mean?" she said.

Well, I thought, it's going to happen, everything's going to be all right.

"Honey, I don't know," I said. She was standing there looking at the picture and I went up behind her and held her in my arms.

"I don't know," I said, kissing her neck. "He's some kind of a genius that's all I know. I'm no genius but I'm nuts about you."

"You're repeating yourself," she said. "Who says he's a genius?"

"He does, for one. And a lot of other people over in the big city."

She walked out of my arms. She went out into the kitchen, snapping on the light beside the door as though she had been there all her life.

"Got any onions?" she said.

"What the hell do you want onions for? Gee, kid, you're gonna drive me crazy in about three minutes."

"I'm gonna make some westerns," she said.

"That's my baby, boys," I said. "She wants a western."

"I spose you want something else," she said.

"All right," I said, what the hell. "There's some onions in this drawer under the refrigerator. Here," I said. "Here's about ten pounds of onions. Is that enough or shall I send out for some more?"

"Got an apron?" she said.

"No, I don't usually go around here in an apron," I said. "Haven't got any apron, Miss Williams. Haven't got any ham either. Can't make no westerns without no ham."

"I'll use bacon," she said. She turned on the gas stove and set the frying pan on.

"That'll be some westerns."

"Well, it'll be food, and I'm hungry."

"Me too, but not for a western."

"How you talk, Sidney."

I made a couple highballs and she worked on the westerns.

"I'm gonna get grease on this dress," she said. "I paid nineteen dollars for it."

"Drink your drink," I said.

I was sitting on a kitchen chair and I pulled her down onto my lap and kissed her. The full treatment.

"All right," she said. "Take it off. Might as well take it off now as later."

"You know what?" I said.

"What?"

"I like you," I said.

If I was one of these Oriental potentates I'd just have the girls in the harem parading around in their slips instead of those filmy long trousers. With their silk stockings on and high-heel shoes — gee but I love to see a girl wandering around the house in her slip. I'd have those harem babies in black slips with pink rosebuds, and in white ones with blue ribbons and lace, and pale green ones with white satin straps, and I'd hire out Molyneux or one of those Paris designers to just think up new kinds of slips, chemises, whatever you want to call them.

I took her dress into the bedroom and hung it up next to the pin-stripe I got wholesale from Jack Stein at Rothstein and Schwartz. A woman's dress without a woman in it is a regular puzzle — you can't find front, back, top or bottom. "Pin-stripe," I said, "this is Miss Williams's dress. You two kids get acquainted."

I picked up a pair of socks off the carpet and stuffed them in the top drawer, lined up my slippers side by side under the bed, turned down the spread, went in the bathroom and brushed my teeth and combed my hair, pulled down the shade, changed the pillowcase and put a clean handkerchief under the pillow, cleaned out the ash tray and set it on the table by the bed, went to the bureau drawer again, and went back to the kitchen.

"I'll come down here sometime and give this stove a good cleaning," Babe said. "It's a mess."

"Why not right now?" I said. "Let's beat the rugs too."

"Here, drink your coffee."

"I wish you'd wear that costume all the time," I said.

"I'd look swell down at the mammoth Sleep Tite plant like this," she said. "What's the matter, don't you like my cooking?"

"Your cooking is swell, baby, but for some peculiar reason I can't get my mind on food right this minute," I said. "Damn funny but I can't seem to concentrate on these westerns."

"You need more salt maybe."

"No I don't need more salt. All I need is more Miss Williams."

She put the dishes in the sink and poured another cup of coffee for herself.

"You drink so much coffee it'll keep you awake," I said.

"Wouldn't that be a shame," she said. She stood in the doorway to my bedroom with the cup of coffee in her hand. One of her straps had slid down over her shoulder. Beautiful, beautiful.

She had that same tantalizing look in her eyes as on the famous night of the union picnic, when she kept looking at me all during Hasler's speech. Through the white silk I could see the dimple in the middle of her belly. God what a picture she made.

She set the coffee cup down and with a wonderful female gesture she began taking pins out of her hair, looking at me all the while with that curious smile of hers, and shook her auburn hair down onto her bare shoulders.

"What're you trying to do, drive me crazy?" I said.

I lit a cigarette off the old one and sat there in my little old kitchen and looked at her, so young, so fair, so goddamn young, so goddamn fair — at that moment the most beautiful girl in all the big wide world full of beautiful girls standing in doorways in their slips. She was one for the history books on that night out in Iowa in my 65-dollar three-room flat. Boys, this two-needle Union Special series 51400 sewing-machine operator was making all those cover girls on *Life* magazine look like imitations that night.

"What're you looking at?" she said. "You drink your coffee. And when you get done, come on in here."

She picked up her cup and went into the bedroom.

So after a while I rinsed out my cup and set it in the sink and went into The Bedroom too.

*Frankly I am more of the aggressive "go-getter" type and can be depended upon to "bring home the bacon" as well as belong to two leading "fraternal" organizations with high standing in one of same.*

— AN APPLICATION

# 9

## The Morning Mail

DEAR FRIEND:

Would you mind filling out the attached coupon and giving us information about yourself as requested below?

This will enable us to tell you more about *your chances* for breaking into a thrilling technical job in TELE-VISION, the fastest growing. . . .

The
Williams and Wilson Press
invites
*Sydney Sorokins*
to examine
for ten days' approval
a copy of the
Plastics Engineers Handbook
prepared by the
Plastics Institute of America


ATTENTION PAYROLL DEPT
For Convenience — Time Saving
and Prevention of Error
USE the NEW
COMBINATION TAX–FINDING BOARD
Models for WEEKLY — BI–WEEKLY and SEMI–
MONTHLY Payroll
Shows NEW Withholding
Slide-guide lines up proper tax deduction . . .
If not completely satisfied . . .
This guarantee . . .
Send your order TODAY


GENTLEMEN:

Are you losing valuable time due to absenteeism caused
by improper seating? Our #320–A Industrial Posture
Chair with swivel or non-swivel posture-type birch ply-
wood seat is adjustable over a 3" range in 8" intervals . . .

[      74      ]

DEAR FRIEND:

Are you satisfied with your flexible couplings and pressure fittings?


ATTENTION:

*Production Manager*

The Ginsberg Applique Scissors are the finest pre-cision-made scissors on the market today with the curved points are ideal for any or all hand-trimming operations, scalloping . . .


*Attention of Manager*

Dear Sir Am Writing you a few lines to Ask a Kindness of you. At present I am confined at the State Prison, Ft. Madison, Ia. If I can Secure employment I can Secure my release on parole in Jan. I have had a little over 2 yrs experience in the Cutting Room of the Shirt Factory here at the Prison . . .


## WE ALL HAVE PROBLEMS
### Are These Yours?

. . . conducting searching and corrosive liquids and gases.

. . . absorption of extreme cycles of vibration, flexation, and vari-plane motions.


Oskaloosa, Iowa
Oct. 26.
DEAR SIR I am writing you at the recomendation of Verna Schiltz (now Mrs. Novak) how sugeted that you

[ 75 ]

might be able to place me. I have had over ten yrs. experence cutting on pajamma and underwer. Reason I am seeking a new place I belive I have reached the limit here as far as I can go in advancment . . .

IS YOUR Business Etiquette helping you get ahead? Here are the answers to hundreds of questions on correct business behavior that come up in everyday . . .

DEAR MR. SUPERINTENDENT:

Do you have surplus, obsolete, or idle electrical power equipment laying around odd corners of your plant gathering dust? Convert this useless equipment into CASH at top price, or get a maximum trade-in allowance of Large Motors, Switchgear, Transformers, Generators (AC & DC), Frequency Changers, Circuit Breakers, Rotary Converters, Variable Voltage Drives, Motor Generator Sets, Control Equipment, Hoists and Pumps. Take Inventory! Write Today! Use the Handy Card!

We sincerely believe you should know more about Ajax #6 electrical tape . . .

*Do You Know?* . . . what it takes to be a good executive?
*Do You Know?* . . . how to get action on executive ideas?
*Do You Know?* . . . the 30 rules for getting things done through people?

. . . and have had two yrs. experience on Union
Special machine sewing belt loops at OK Pants plant in
Keokuk Mr Solomon superntendent can give reference
am seeking enployment due to . . .


*Att:* MAINTENANCE SUPERVISOR:
DINA–MITE Super Strength Drain Cleaner is guaranteed to open any drain clogged with grease, sludge, soap
accumulations of hair, lint, grease, paper and cigarette
butts or any other material capable of being dissolved.
The furious churning of this boiling solvent . . .


"Say Mabel," I said. "How's your husband's regularity
problem? Has he got that licked yet? Here's something
I got an ad on in the mail called Dina-Mite Super Strength
Drain Cleaner, I'll bet it's just what he needs. Says it is
guaranteed to open any drain clogged with sludge, grease,
baling wire, bolts, nuts, screws, slag, or mine tailings."
"I must say it is a change in this office to hear somebody making jokes and wisecracks and like that," Mabel
said. "Now Mr. Coots he was a fine man, always treated
me fine, but you couldn't say he was very much on the
humorous and comical side. I set behind him and Mrs.
Coots one time up at the old Majestic theater that is now
the R.K.O. and it was Don Dixon and company on the
stage well it was the funniest show honestly I ever saw
in my life I do believe. That Don was the craziest thing,
had the whole audience in stitches, ole Mrs. Lena Kauf-
man up in a box got to laughing so she nearly had a fit —
had to leave the theater — took her home in a taxicab

[     77     ]

which was rare for them days; oh this must of been 1928 or so, maybe 1926, and that night she had a stroke never left the house again from that night. Buried her on St. Patrick's day the following year. Anyway I for myself was doubled up I'm telling you that Don Dixon could put an audience in the hospital from the laughing if he didn't stop his antrics in time. And in front of me through it all set Mr. Coots just taking it all in like it was some education movie on the life of the Eskimos or something. 'Well Mr. Coots,' I says to him next day, 'I seen you at the show last night, in fact I set right behind you. How did you like the show?' 'Excellent,' he says. 'I enjoyed it very much. Dixon has a lot of talent.' 'Well,' I says, 'I din't see you laughing very much, I thought maybe you was bored with the performance.' 'Certainly not,' he says. 'I enjoyed myself thoroughly and so did Mrs. Coots.'"

"How'd Coots get along with Mr. Hasler?" I said, dumping all the third-class mail in the wastebasket.

"They got along very peculiar. They didn't neither of them like the other, in fact couldn't stand the sight. So you see it was eighteen years of hell around here in some ways."

"You got yesterday's production figures yet?"

"I'll have them in five minutes, *with* the cutting reports," Mabel said. The morning sunshine was pouring in through the venetian blinds, and our office was warm and cheerful. The sewing machines were humming out in the plant and one of them out there was Babe's and she was there and soon I would walk through the plant and I would see her.

"Yes," Mabel said, "Mr. Coots use to hold himself in with Mr. Hasler, but sometimes it was too much. One time $\frac{3}{12}$ dozen silk pajamas was short. We never did find them pajamas, pure dye silk they was, and somehow $\frac{3}{12}$ dozen got lost in this plant. You ask me, it was that Vernon Putts we had on the elevator. Anyway Mr. Hasler just made Mr. Coots's life miserable over them $\frac{3}{12}$ dozen silk pajamas, he even implied Mr. Coots was careless, unresponsible, and all that, he was just terrible about it. One morning Mr. Hasler was on him again with some rude remark another about the silk pajamas Mr. Coots says to him he says, 'Myron Hasler your old man used to cut my father's hair and shave him. I remember you from the Third Ward School. Now if I hear another word out of you about those missing pajamas I'm walking out. You can pull this stuff on the stenographers and the elevator boys and others too miserable to fight back but not on me.'

"Oh that was exciting I tell you," she went on. " 'And moreover,' says Mr. Coots, 'you'll have a sweet time finding a superintendent at the bargain price you got me for.' "

"Sounds kinda ridiculous to me," I said. "Grown-up men."

"Anyway there was no more mention of the lost $\frac{3}{12}$ dozen silks. Here's your production for yesterday. Up a little."

I was interested to hear that the legendary Mr. Coots had thrown in Hasler's face the fact that Hasler's father had applied the hot towels and bay rum to Coots Senior. Good old Coots!

"Coots must have been some old boy," I said. "I think

[ 79 ]

I'll go out and put some lilacs on his grave on Memorial Day."

"Oh he's buried out in Mosalem Township someplace in some little country churchyard. His folks was wealthy farmers out there. His brother Elmer Coots owns most of the township though he drinks terrible. He had a bad fall a few years ago they say he was lit and since then the boys has took over the farms and Elmer mostly sets around. Well, I hope you and Miss Williams had a nice time Friday night, Otto Pancratz told Bert he seen you two over at the Sixty-Six just more than hitting it off."

"That was a mighty quick switch from Elmer Coots to me and my four-star romance," I said. "I suppose Otto gave Bert our dinner menu and a description of my necktie, too."

"No, he didn't, but he did say you was mighty chummy with the floor show. Said you had this floor-show singer right at your table with you."

"Oh that's nothing. I know the guy that feeds the lions at the Brookfield Zoo, too," I said.

Then the phone rang and it was Brokamp, the traffic manager, and he says when are we going to get some of those number 318's, he is holding up a lot of orders for them and it is a pity because they were sold for October first delivery and here it is the sixth and no 318's and how can we stay in business with nothing coming out of the factory and what's the matter up there anyway? So I told him the goods had come in three weeks late to start with but we had put a red number on it and rushed it through and they would have it by the end of the week.

Well we're gettin cancellations he says and I says that is a damn shame but we can't cut the cloth until we get it and he ought to talk to Jack Smith the piece-goods buyer. So he roared on some more and hung up and by that time there was two pale anemic-looking fifteen-year-old girls standing in front of my desk, sore at life on the farm and in town for the day to look for a job. We weren't hiring any of this brand of talent so I told them to leave their names and they went out sad.

"Oh they'll find work up at the packing house or one of the dime stores," Mabel said. "Let somebody else struggle with that kinda help. Now what I'd like to see waltz in here is a big hefty girl who we could put onto that folding job. We could use another folder since that fool Delaney quit though I must admit she was a whiz of a folder."

And then the union chairman came in and we discussed old Mrs. Theobald's compensation problems for a half an hour. This union chairman of ours was the poorest cutter on the staff, but he had read a book on elocution once upon a time and how that bird could talk. He could put in a whole half hour discussing a busted window shade, always bringing in what little he knew of the history of the labor movement, with elaborate and inaccurate emphasis on the famous Triangle Shirtwaist affair. It was no use to try to cut him off after five minutes by barking at him in a hearty and jovial way: "O.K. Frank, we will take care of that shade right away. Thanks for calling my attention to it," because he was getting paid by the union for whatever time he spent in discussing the window shade and if there was one thing in life he hated it was running a cutting machine, whereas the big love of his life was this big long inexhaustible string of baloney he dished out by the goddamn hour.

This Mrs. Theobald's compensation was his baby — the old girl had got balled up somehow on her unemployment compensation when she had been laid off for five days, months before, and the whole affair had gotten so tangled up by now it was worse than the Chinese budget and would never be solved.

"So as I see it," he was saying after twenty-five minutes, "you got to look at the case from all or various angles of the situation in order to elucidate the different complexeries of the point of view not only of the *worker's* point of view but the unemployment board likewise as well as the company. Now the legal rights of the worker here in this case looks to me like they have been entirely overlooked considering the fact Theobald has got legal claim on the compensation in question even though she failed to file claim until twenny-eight fiscal days later which of course she was in the wrong but on the other hand what was the Unemployment set up for in the first place it was just for such contingency as this and the fact they got no rule covering it got no bearing on the case as I see it and although she quit and was rehired in the intravening period certainly don't legally according to the statue books of the State of Iowa indicate in any way shape or form the fact the worker in question was culpably to blame since she was ignorant of the . . ."

Another ten minutes and he paused for breath and said, "I don't want to take up your valuable time but . . ."

[     82     ]

And he started to launch off into some more of the same old hash but I jumped up and said I had a meeting with Hasler and would have to discuss Theobald again some other time. So he went back to his daily contest with himself of seeing how slow he could cut a board of fifty-dozen pajamas and how many pockets, backs, collars, etc., he could damage slightly. As far as he was concerned the interview had been a success; nothing had been accomplished and he could look forward to another Theobald meeting after a few days.

However as he was leaving he turned and said, "Theobald and all that aside, though, we got to do something about this here 7½ cents. I suppose Mr. Hasler told you that Rubenstein will be here next week, din't he?"

"Yeah," I said (Hasler never having mentioned the subject in any way shape or form), "I believe he did mention it."

"You know," he said, staring at his feet (he was a great shoelace and ceiling inspector, always looking down or up, never at you), "all the rest of the industry got the increase September the first and here it is October and we ain't even got Hasler to talk about it yet. First he was away, then he was sick, then he was too busy, by God this has got to get settled." He studied the ceiling. "Well anyways," he said, "I'll see you later on this Theobald case."

"So Rubenstein is coming next week," I said when he had gone. "That'll be good. I better buy a bottle of vitamin pills and get in shape for the Battle of the Century."

"Now you take Jake Rubenstein," Mabel said. "To me he's the easiest man in the world to get along with. But oh

Mr. Hasler, you know he's death on Jews. He just don't care a bit for Rubenstein."

"That's a tough spot to be in: Down on Jews in the garment industry. There aren't more than a half dozen gentiles in the whole club, whether it's piece goods, machinery, or manufacturing."

"Why don't you end the agony and take a walk through the plant and have a look at Babe Williams and cheer up?" Mabel said. "And while you're at it take a look at that new girl on buttonholes and see if she's putting them in upside down or sideways."

"O.K. teacher," I said. "And you get your pencil out and figure how we put 7½ cents on the piece rates."

"You got quite a case on that girl, haven't you?" she said.

"Yes," I said. "I think I'll ask her if I can carry her books home after school."

"You're quite a change from Mr. Coots," she said.

"I can see that," I said.

*The real interest in manufacturing is the intensity of production, the number of garments per square foot that can be produced.*

— THE PROGRESSIVE SEWING ROOM

# 10

THE RUSH SEASON was on. Anybody raised in the garment trade, and most people in it were, knows and loves the rush season like the sailor loves departure day, when the ship comes alive and everybody is running every which way and the tugs come alongside and the captain appears on the bridge.

Out in the plant was a crazy scene of activity, so that an outsider coming in would have said everyone concerned had gone mad and that all the principles of scientific management so dear to our hearts had been dumped into the elevator shaft, and that confusion, inefficiency, and outrageous costs would almost immediately drive the fat-headed management into bankruptcy.

The desk girl was hollering at the elevator boy, the elevator boy was slamming trucks around furiously and whistling, giggling, roaring with laughter, snapping his gum and having a whale of a time. At one end of the room, behind the big long counter called "the desk," where the desk girls struggled at laying out the bundles for the operators and kept answering the constantly ringing telephone, the piled-up cut lots ready for the machines were stacked in apparently unidentifiable chaos.

"We didn't get them buttons yet," says the forelady, rushing up and squawking in my ear.

"They're in transit," I said. "You'll just have to set the lot aside until they get here."

"For my part," says one of the instructors to me in a cold and dismal tone, "I never seen such junk come out of a cutting room in all my life. Them cutters must of went on a two-week drunk I never seen such terrible cutting, I blieve they are chopping the sleeves out with an ax. My girls can't do nothing with them sleeves why Verna Mae Schlesinger has been bawling her eyes out all morning. If she quits we'll be in a fine pickle of fish and then they'll wanna know where our sleeve setters are at. Call *them* cutters? They couldn't get by with that stuff at Imperial

[    86    ]

Glove and Mitten, by golly. They'd be out in the street holding up the telephone poles."

"I'll go down and raise hell with 'em, Gert," I said. "Get the work out. Pay time-work if you have to, but get it out. We gotta have pajamas going down that old chute. I'm counting on *you*."

"For a dime I'd go back to Imperial," she said. She wouldn't go back even if she could. She was having the time of her life.

"You can't go back, Gert. They're busted and out of business," I said. "Anyway, I'm counting on you. You know how to get the work out of these gum-chewers."

"You talk to them cutters," she said. "Them bums."

It is mighty cheerful in a garment plant going wide open. The lights are bright and the sewing machines are working out themes by Stravinsky; it's warm and lively; the blonde table tops gleam; the needles are punching their way to glory 4500 stitches a minute. Telephones are ringing, the elevator gate is banging, voices are raised and the whole room is filled with women, all shapes and sizes, fat, thin, possible, impossible, goofy, semi-goofy, happy, sad, bouncing brunettes, silver threads among the gold, slap-happy bobby socks kids, old grousers with eight kids, and then the queens, always about two or three queens on each floor.

You have different kinds of true queens in a garment factory. One type is the speedy number with upswept hairdo who wears fancy earrings to work and when you see her out at some night club in the evening she has on this fantastic hat so everybody looks at her and she is with some slicker who dances all the hot numbers in three-quarter time and has a little moustache. Then another common type is the regal girl, tall and stately, who walks very carefully and when you see her out at night she has on a black dress and some pearls and is with a C.P.A. or some bird who owns a garage. (This type is so refined they never get married.) Then there are the blooming beautiful corn-fed girl from the country, with pink cheeks, blue eyes, and an assortment of skirts and well-filled tricky shirtwaists from J. C. Penney. Conversation with the corn-fed beauty is likely to slow down to a dead stop after twenty minutes, but she makes up for it in other ways.

On the fourth floor of my busy little factory there were two queens: a quiet brunette with olive skin and enormous dark eyes named Delores Paradiso, who put buttonholes in the flys of men's pajamas with a genteel air as though she were pouring tea at the Junior League, and Babe Williams, my freckled, auburn-haired tornado who operated a Union Special 51400 and could set more sleeves in an eight-hour day than any operator between Council Bluffs and Columbus.

"How's the new buttonhole girl coming along?" I asked the forelady, leaning on the desk by the telephone and surveying the floor. A hundred feet away, across the heads of the other operators, I could see the glow of Babe's lovely hair under the fluorescent lights.

"Well, she won the mayonnaise prize, that's all I know about her yet," she said.

"Did you say the mayonnaise prize?" I said.

"Oh she comes from out in the state someplace on one

of them big farms out there and she won this mayonnaise prize at the State Fair in Des Moines last year so she told Mae Weidenbacher."

"Well, the buttonhole job oughta be a cinch for a mayonnaise champion," I said. "But how is she taking to it?"

"Real good, so far. Seems to like it all right. Anyway most of these farm girls are so anxious to get into town and off the farm and away from cooking and baking for a bunch of hungry farm hands and getting no credit for it either, that they would do most anything just so they can stay in town and walk up and down Main Street and hang around the roller rink and the dance hall."

"Is she coming up any?" That means are her earnings on piece rates coming up.

"Not much yet. But she will. She's strong like most of these farm kids. She could pick up that machine and throw it across the street if she had a mind to."

"I hope she don't get that notion then," I said. The phone rang. The forelady answered it.

"That you Mr. Novak?" she said. "Listen, I want you to come down here and look at the fronts on lot 316 cut 6. Them cutters of yours must of all been out to another stag party. These fronts look like they was cut out with an ax. The notches are an inch off. Come and see for yourself."

She hung up. Then she picked up the phone again.

I looked down through the grove of women towards Babe.

"Listen honey," the forelady said to the operator. "Where's that machinist at? I had a call in for him for thirty-five minutes now. I got Charlene Winkler setting here with her machine busted down and she's holding up the whole works. Try him again, honey. He's probly on his hinder down in the boiler room smoking cigarettes."

"Gimme the phone," I said.

"Hello," I said. "This is Sorokin. Please tell the machinist I said for him to get up here as soon as he can. Fourth floor. Winkler's machine."

"Thanks," the forelady said. One of the desk girls squeezed past me carrying a huge bundle of pajama pants. A skinny girl came up to the desk. Her hair was up in pin curlers. Big date tonight.

"Gimme a needle," she said to a desk girl. "I just busted another."

"Jeez, you're sure rough on the needles," the desk girl said.

"Who's missing down there at that empty felling machine?" I said.

"Mitzi Bartlett," the forelady said.

The phone rang and she answered it.

"No we didn't get that shartroose piping yet and we're holding the whole lot up. All I can get out of them is it's in transit. Must be in transit from Paris, France." She hung up.

"What's the matter with Bartlett?" I said.

"Well now that's quite a story. Excuse me a minute." She got a new spool of green thread and took it down the aisle to one of the pocket setters. All over the floor you could spot the brilliant and horrible colors of the famous Lovers-On-Parade number.

"Well now about Bartlett," she said when she got back.

"She took it into her head to go on this egg diet all the girls have been talking about so much, it was wrote up in the Sunday supplement of some Chicago paper and Josie Hughes you wouldn't remember her she is over there with her sister now and working in the Reliance Plant, Josie sent this clipping in to one of the girls and they talked about it quite a bit so Mitzi decided to try it. She is terrible fat you know but has a cute face and would be a real cute girl if she was to remove some of the excess flesh so to speak. So she gets going on the egg diet and as she is not fond of hardly any styles of egg it is pretty hard going for the poor kid but anyway, one type egg she doesn't mind so much is hard-boiled. Well you know what hard-boiled eggs does — and in a few days she was tied up something awful, constipated I mean. The darn fool she might of known it would happen. What do you think of that?"

"I don't know what to think. What's the rest of it?"

"Why my god she's been off work for a week. The poor child is in a terrible condition why she's home for six days now and she has to sit in the bathtub in hot water four times a day."

"I hope she will get out of the tub and back to us next week," I said. "How many pounds did she lose?"

"Lost nine pounds but now setting around home all day with the icebox handy she probly put it all back again and then some."

The Deaf Mute came up to the desk for a spool of black thread. She went away.

"How come your production was off Thursday?" I said. "Are the girls having trouble with this new number?"

"Well, truth to tell there's something funny going on," she said. "Seems like the girls have just let down. Not all of them, but some of the best girls on the floor are falling way down. I can't figure it out."

"Who, for example?"

"Anna Mae Rayburn for one. Her quota is forty dozen and she slipped way down to twenny-eight dozen. Usually she hits near fifty. And Ramona Katz is off about ten dozen. And the fellers are way down too. But they're not the worst."

"Who's the worst then?"

"Babe Williams, if you must know. One of our best operators. She usually sets around forty-five dozen sleeves a day and she's way down below thirty. She's movin so slow she seems paralyzed."

"What's it all about? Is she sick?"

"No she ain't sick. She looks the same as ever. She ain't sick because I ast her."

"That's bad," I said. "What's going on anyway?"

"Mr. Sorokin," she said. "Did you hear about this 7½ cents?"

"Yeah," I said. "I heard about it."

"That 7½ cents, that's why Babe Williams and the rest are just dragging around and hanging back."

"We got a slowdown on our hands, hey?"

"We sure have," she said.

"My but it used to be peaceful when I worked in the cutting room," I said. "All I had to worry about was my work and my machine."

"Yes but now you're the superintendent," she said.

The telephone began to ring again and I went out onto the floor and walked down between the sewing machines and the operators and the bright patterns of Sleep Tite pajamas in process, The Nite Wear for Men of Bedroom Discrimination.

*No knowledge of music is necessary, merely
place kazoo to lips and hum your favorite tune.*

# 11

"Now LOOK HERE at this five-cent blue," says
Babe's old man. "I wouldn't be surprised if I'm the only
collector in Junction County that has two complete mint
sets of the 1901 Pan-Americans."

"What is that on there? What is that supposed to be?"
I said.

"That's the bridge at Niagara Falls. Now here, see on the ten-cent yellow-brown and black — that's an ocean steamship. That stamp right there is worth six dollars."

"Can you beat that!" I said.

"Now the eight-cent brown-violet and black, that's worth about four and a quarter."

"I like this two-cent red and black with the locomotive on it," I said.

"Carmine and black, you mean. That's carmine and black they call it. That's actually only worth about forty cents."

"Well, I like it anyway," I said. "I like that stamp."

"Well, there you see that's where experience comes in. Like in everything else you can't beat experience," he says. "Now stamps are one of the most complicated subjects known. You take a stamp expert and you'll find a mighty shrewd, keen-minded individual nearly every time. Now I have been studying stamps for years and I think I have covered the ground pretty thoroughly. So you see where you made your big mistake here is, you just went ahead and picked a stamp by the looks of the thing alone. You can't go by that. Now this particular stamp I happen to know . . ."

"For heaven's sake, Pop, let him alone," Babe said swishing into the room in a new dress from the La Parisian and a quart of perfume. "Let Sid alone. Give the stamps a rest."

"What's the matter with the stamps may I ask?" he said. "How many collectors around here have a complete set of mint Columbians?"

"Oh ye gods," Babe said.

[      95      ]

She put on her black tailored coat with the fur collar and kissed Pop bye-bye. I looked around the room at the circulating oil heater and the starched curtains and the upright piano with a marbleized clock on it that struck the quarter hours, and at Mr. Williams sitting beside me on the overstuffed couch with the stamp album on his knees. He was a big man with a big Hamilton railroad watch that had big black numbers on it, and he had a white moustache and wore an old maroon smoking jacket.

"Maybe you would like to see my model railroad," he said. "Just take a minute?"

"Now Pop," Babe said, looking in the mirror and patting her hair aimlessly.

They will tell you all kinds of things, these old men. They will tell you about some postage stamp, they will tell you thousands of things, all of them boring as hell. It is not so much the subject is boring, but these old boys after they get past fifty why only one in a hundred can say anything at all without you wanting to fall sound asleep within about two minutes. Brother, are they stupefying.

Then all you can do is look out the window, select a piece of Juicy Fruit gum, or change the subject to Schliemann's exploits at Mycenae. Oh don't breathe a word to me about fathers with postage-stamp albums, because I've been there and back a dozen times or more, with no refreshment other than a warm bottle of cream soda, and I can tell you it's torture, it's the kind of torture a young man has to get used to: listening to these played-out old boys determined to shove you down over your ears into the mud with their superior knowledge. If it isn't stamps it's politics — if not politics it's accounting — or baseball or African violets or deer-hunting or the Ford Motor Co. or how to lick Wall Street or what is the Matter in Washington. There is no hesitation waltz about it — they are perfectly willing to tell you all about everything and all FREE, FREE, FREE, just clip the coupon and stand there with your mouth open. Just keep saying No Kidding, Ain't That Wonderful, Just Imagine, The Hell You Say, I'll Be Darned, Can You Beat That, Is That A Fact, and Have You Got A Pencil I Want To Write That Down.

"Well, you got the full treatment on the stamps," Babe said, when we had got into the car and started rolling down the street where there were a few leaf piles smoldering in the gutters as a signal of the fall season. "I'm sorry I was so long."

"That's all right," I said. "You ought to hear my old man on the subject of Mischa Elman."

"Who is he?" Babe said, as we pulled up to a stop light and watched the cars filled with human vegetables soar past us on the cross traffic in the early evening, to various uninteresting destinations.

"A violin player," I said. "To hear my dad talk about him you would get the impression he should be elected President of the World."

Will you be there when I need you my dearest Love, beside the Shalimar restaurant in South Chicago, pale hands I loved near the cab stand? Will you always be there, and if you are, will you be any help to me, may I ask, or will you be playing Canasta and kicking about the gas bill?

"You're awfully funny Sidney," she said, "but don't you ever think about that mess over at the plant?"

"No," I said. "Shall we eat at the Wander Inn or the Romance?"

"Don't you even *care* about it?" says the Babe.

"This is my night out," I said. "You look wonderful."

"What are you going to do about this thing anyway?"

"Baby, I don't wanna talk about all that now. Can't we just talk about you?"

"God forbid. No, we've got to get straightened out on this or quit going out."

"What! After the other night?"

"Never mind about the other night."

We passed over the east end of the bridge and a long freight from St. Paul was hammering down the tracks beneath us bound for Chicago.

"Babe, you drive me crazy the way you talk," I said. "Don't talk like that." I grabbed her nice warm hand.

"Oh Sid, you're crazy already," she said.

A nice theme on which to enter the Romance, a dump where some fathead played the piano accordion all over the place until you wanted to murder the bastard.

I kissed her in the car but it wasn't much of a kiss.

"What's the matter, you got religion or something?" I said.

"Let's go in and get at the food," she said.

We got a swell table next to the kitchen where the aroma of French fries would knock you out if you weren't in shape.

"I guess you wanna talk about it," I said. "O.K. I was

*raised* in the labor movement. My papa came here in 1919 from Russia and went into the steel mills in Gary when it was tough, baby, tougher than anything anybody knows who wasn't there."

"Two bourbon and water," she said to the waitress.

"You hear me?" I said.

"I hear you."

"I know what the hell is going on," I said. "So we get into a big mess. O.K., I been in messes before. I've been in one mess after another for the last ten years. I know all about messes. I love 'em."

"This is different, Mr. Superintendent," she said. "Your fine noble friend Hasler is going to get it, but good. We are all pretty sore, Sidney."

"I'm sure tired of this superintendent routine," I said. "Do I look like a superintendent right now or what?"

"And Sidney, you'll be all mixed the hell up in it whether you like it or not. There's gonna be a battle, I keep telling you. You on one side and me on the other. I'm a *machine operator*, Sid. You're the boss. You and that silly son of a bitch Hasler."

"I could sure use some sympathy instead of a lot of rough stuff when I take my girl friend out in the evening," I said.

"Now I'm your girl friend already," she said.

"What the hell were we doing the other night if you're not my girl friend?"

"You've sure got that on the brain," she said. "Whyn't you worry a little more about your career and forget about 'the other night'?"

"I'll take care of the career all right," I said. "Listen, Small Town," I said. "I went through four years Gary High School and I've been taking night school, correspondence, and extension courses ever since. I'm gonna make it, if it kills me. Of all the bright boys I went with what is the outcome up to date? My good friend Joe Wyzanski who was gonna set the world on fire is driving a milk truck. My friend Frank Novak who stood highest in the class and won all the trigonometry prizes is running his old man's little old fruit store. Johnny Freiburg, the big basketball hero with his picture in the *Tribune* twice, is in the steel mill, has five kids already, and lives in a flat over a pool hall. There's only three of us looking good — Kosciuszko painting some kind of goofy pictures over at the Art Institute. Stan Marco running around the country doing three shows a night in the punk night clubs. And me.

"They all thought Kosciuszko was nuts in school, but now he's getting up there and the others are making milk collections. That's a rugged life over there — you small-town kids don't know what it's like. Being born in a steel town is like being born with a ton of rock on top of you. You got to fight your way out. While you kids over here in the sticks are studying the birds and the bees and pressing flowers in the family album, us roughnecks are throwing paving bricks and trying to get a breath of fresh air.

"I been through it all. And I didn't end up on no milk wagon, or in a steel mill, or soda jerk or movie usher or sidewalk bum. Sure I come up out of the cutting room, but

[    100    ]

I made it my own way, and I'm glad I'm here. And it's not funny. Not to me anyway."

"Sidney, Sidney," she said. "That's all very well and you had one hell of a time fighting with the polacks and . . ."

"Poles, not polacks," I said.

". . . with the Polish boys and your old man in the steel mill and you fought your way out of it, maybe, like you say. But as long as you're the superintendent and I'm a member of the Associated Garment Workers you and I are going to be always getting into a big mixup." She picked up her highball and drained it.

"Why don't you quit?" I said. "Then we won't have no more trouble you and I."

"Very funny," she said. "Get me another bourbon," she said. "Where can I go in this town and make a dollar and a half an hour? Do you think I work because I love sewing so much it thrills me to sit on my ass at a machine eight hours a day setting sleeves on your lousy old Sleep Tite pajamas?"

"Cut it out, honey," I said. "Damn it, don't let's fight."

"Sure, my dad makes good money on the railroad and what's he do with it? Spends it on those damn postage stamps and this wonderful model railroad of his and the leftover on War Bonds. He's got so many War Bonds they need an annex on the bank to hold them. When I used to ask him for some money for a dress he used to give me five dollars. You know what a locomotive costs on his famous model railroad? Seventy-five dollars. So I went to work. And I'm still a union member and you're the boss."

The accordion player was going wide open on "Nola."
All the jerks were staring at him empty-headed.

"This is a swell date," I said. "One of the swellest dates
I ever had."

She took her new highball as soon as the waitress set it
down and drank half of it.

"You're sure walloping that stuff tonight," I said.

"Sometimes I do that," she said.

"O.K. then," I said.

"It was me that started the slowdown in the plant. You
know that don't you?" she said. "I started it and the rest
are gonna follow me. Well, why don't you say something
about it?" She leaned across the table and stuck her puss
right close up to mine. She wanted to fight but all I wanted
to do was kiss her. "And quit looking like a sick calf,"
she said. "I started the slowdown. We're out to ruin your
precious 'production record' unless that big pal of yours
Hasler gives us this 7½ cents. What do you think of that,
*boy friend?*"

"I don't wanna think about it," I said. I drained my highball.

"You *got* to think about it, you sap."

"Darling, it'll all turn out all right," I said. "You're
making too much of it."

"Lay off that 'darling' crap," says the queen. "Was your
father in the steel strike? Do you think he made too much
of it?"

"Lay off, kid, lay off," I said.

"Oh god, let's dance," she said.

She may have been sore but she didn't show it in her

[      102      ]

dancing. The squeeze-box artist was playing "Near You."

" 'Near You,' " she said. "You know, I kinda like this piece."

"If you get any nearer to me right here on the floor," I said, "they'll call the cops."

"You're funnier than the boys I'm used to dating," she said.

I can't stand that word "dating." I don't like "formal" either when they mean evening dress. I have all kinds of queer prejudices — specialties like that to torture myself with. Right about this time everybody was saying "out of this world," probably the crummiest popular phrase that ever hit the country. Everything was "out of this world." Everybody said it constantly and they all thought they were being bright and clever. Whenever anybody was real hot on something, whether it was some new disc by Armstrong or a new kind of pickle relish or auto chains, they just gave up any idea of using their goddamn brains to give an accurate description and burbled, "Oh it's out of this world." Would make a good man throw up.

"How many other boys you used to going out with, anyway?" I said. The one-man musical sensation turned on "Linger Awhile" and we danced some more. We got along fine, Babe was O.K. on the floor. I'm not so slick but I like to dance. Babe's perfume and hair and her stuff against me were killing me. I was glad the storm was over, for now at least.

"Oh I've got about three dozen on the string," she said.

"I don't doubt it," I said. "But I think I better do something about that."

"Oh you do, do you?"

"Uh huh," I said.

We danced for a while and the accordion player wore out and went over to the bar for a beer and we went back past the table where the girls from an insurance office were giving a party for one of their fellow underwriters who was about to get married, and we sat down, undecided, in our nook on the fringe of French-fried potatoland.

"I'm sorry about what I said before," she said, and commanded a sizzling steak from the waitress, who was sore at life in general and not sizzling.

"That's all right," I said. "It'll be one swell big All-American mess, but we'll lick it one way or another. I'll have the sizzling also," I said to the waitress.

"You want the French fries or the home fries? You want coffee now or later? You wanna shrimp cocktail? You care for a drink from the bar?" the waitress said in a tedious frame of mind. She looked from side to side around the room as though seeking more aristocratic trade.

"Two shrimp and two bourbon and water," Babe said, giving me the foot and partial leg under the table. And the waitress went away, gliding carefully and with refinement between the tables.

"I'm still gonna do what I said," she said. "I mean about the slowdown."

"I know you are, Babe. Don't worry about it, kid. It's Hasler's mess. Go ahead and slow down to six bundles."

"And if there's a strike, I'll be right out there on the sidewalk carrying a banner or whatever you carry."

"The Associated doesn't have strikes," I said. "There won't be any strike."

"Don't be so sure, smarty. Your pal Hasler is a stubborn old buck."

"A 'fighter,' he calls it."

" 'Fighter' ——," she said.

"Such language for a girl so beautiful," I said. "Where did you learn such words?"

"I live on Railroad Avenue, Sidney, not up on Summit Boulevard with the Watsons."

"These Watsons, they must be some stuff," I said. "All I hear around this town is the Watsons."

"Oh they're just like anybody, I suppose," Babe said. I was studying her eyes in the imperfect light, and thinking vaguely of her old man's stamp collection. "But they've got the money. That's nice when you have all the money."

"Yeah, money," I said.

"All that money," she said. "And she's so damn stupid."

"Who's so damn stupid?"

The waitress arrived, mincing with gentility, and set the drinks in front of us as though they were contaminated.

"Celeste. Celeste Watson," Babe said. "She's got everything, but she's batty as hell they say." She knocked off half the beverage in a gulp.

"She's supposed to be out of this world," she said.

"Do me a favor, will you baby, and give up the 'out of this world'?" I said.

"God but you're difficult," she said.

"Maybe so. But just give up 'out of this world,' will you?

You've got a brain inside that beautiful head so just abandon the use of that dull expression, how about it?"

"Let's you and me give the whole thing up," she said. "You'd be better off with Watson or some wonder girl who didn't say the wrong thing all the time. Me, I'm just too goddamn dumb for your aristocratic taste. You're so big and smart and wonderful. You heel."

The sizzlers arrived presently and we ate, glaring at each other over the A-1 Sauce. It was a swell dinner.

"How's your steak?" I said.

"Rotten, how's yours, big shot," she said.

*"How could you marry off your daughter to a schafskopf like Federman?"* he asked.

*"It was a love match, Noblestone,"* Zudrowsky explained. *"She falls in love with him, and he falls in love with her. So naturally he ain't no businessman, y'understand, because you know as well as I do, Noblestone, a businessman ain't got no time to fool away on such nonsense."*

— POTASH AND PERLMUTTER

# 12

"Nothing wonderful is gonna happen to us in here," I said, "so let's go over to the International."

"It's ten o'clock," she said. "I better go home. I got to build up my strength for the picket line."

"Oh come on over to the International," I said. "It's quiet in there and the drinks are not cut with gasoline and whenever you want to pull out, O.K. with me. You can have a cordial or some three-colored drink and we can talk for a while or just sit."

"All right. Let's get out of here fast before we hear 'Nola' again." That's my Babe with the green eyes.

"Oh now," I said, "I think he's just out of this world."

"Come on, smarty, pay up and let's go."

We crossed the street and walked up a block and all the stars were out but making a poor show against the neon lights.

I don't know where they found the back bar in this International bar — it looked like Salvador Dali and L. Frank Baum had collaborated on it. It had more carving, clusters of 25-watt bulbs, art glass panels, and marble columns than I ever saw before outside of a picture book. It also had beveled glass mirrors and genuine statuary works and every so often there were real dollar bills pasted to the surface of the bar and varnished over so the rubes were all the time about to pick them up with their change.

"This is Watson territory," Babe said. "This is where all the big stuff comes."

"I like it here anyway," I said. I had found my way in here one lonesome night when I was first in town. This bar was owned by some big operator named Joyce. He was quite the stuff in town — owned another joint three or four miles out in the country that catered to the farm trade, and he made big money, so they said, off the two places. Of course when they say "big money" in a small town, you don't know what to think.

"Oh she's got money," Mabel would say about some old

girl in the plant. "She married Cletus Vandergraf and he died six months later and left her well fixed."

"How much money would that be?" I would say.

"Oh my lands, she's rich," she would say. "Why he must have left her five thousand on the insurance and the house too."

Anyway this man Joyce was actually "fixed," drove a big car, played golf with all the best real estate men and bankers — so I guess the operation was a success.

"What do you want?" I said to Babe.

"Just another bourbon and water," she said. "I don't like these green drinks and all that."

"Bourbon and water, and a brandy," I said to the bartender. I knew him, his name was Marc, an old-timer. Could tell you more stories about Scarlatti and the Chicago booze-runners of the 20's than old Al himself.

"How do you like it here by now?" he said. "Gettin use to it yet?"

"I like it O.K.," I said.

"How's Hasler?" he said.

"He's O.K.," I said.

"Well, we got winter on our hands now," he said. "I don't look forward to it none."

"I'll go along with you on that," Babe said.

"These winters over in here, these hard winters are bad, friend. Different in the big city. Just as cold and miserable but it don't seem so bad somehow. Over here in the long grass you want to go crazy by spring." He wore a high collar and starched cuffs with cameo cuff links.

"I'm too busy to go crazy," I said.

"That's what you think," Babe said — another crummy expression.

Marc went down to the other end of the bar. Business was slow.

"Don't look now and break your neck," Babe said, "but there she is."

"There who is?" I said.

"Celeste Watson," she said. "Over there at that table by the rubber plant."

Another of Joyce's ideas was shrubbery around the place. There were potted plants and even a potted palm. During the holiday rush they said he had cut flowers on the bar and orchids for the ladies. By such tricks he attracted all the best trade for miles around.

"I can see her in the mirror," I said. "She doesn't look so hot from here."

"She doesn't look too hot from anyplace," Babe said. "But she's a Watson."

And another woman having come into the conversation, she unconsciously pulled a mirror about one inch square out of her bag and began to give herself the once-over.

"Well she's got class, anyway," I said.

"Oh my god," Babe said.

"She's nothing much on looks," I said quickly.

"You can say that again," she said.

This was going to be a long up-grade pull with this red-head, getting her to give up the canned heat and use her head. "You can say that again!" There'll be Some Changes Made, here, if this thing gets serious, I thought. And it's likely to. The Babe and her freckles and green eyes is look-

ing so much better than the Watson doll that I am beginning to realize in some dim male way just what I have
located over here in the brush.

"Excuse me a minute, Sidney," Babe said, and got down
from the bar stool and walked back toward the ladies' room.
The boys with Watson watched her go by. The guys at
the other tables also.

"Ready for another?" Marc said.

"O.K.," I said. "The same."

He brought the bottle over and poured me a Hennessey.
Then he took Babe's glass and dumped it and made another highball and brought it back.

"Can I buy you a drink?" I said.

He looked up and down the bar and out through the big
plate-glass window into the street.

"Ordinarily," he said, "I never take a drink while I'm
working. But the prospects of the winter season has got me
so low in my mind I do believe I will." He poured himself
a very small Hennessey.

"You married?" I asked.

The other two bartenders were taking care of the customers for the moment.

"My feet are killing me," he said. "Am I married? Four
times I jumped into the bramble patch, and the latest is the
worst of the lot. Why man I'm so scratched up and bunged
up from matrimony I feel like one of these here vaudeville
husbands that comes out on the stage all black and blue and
all over court plaster."

"It don't show much," I said.

"This latest one was supposed to own three farms in

[    111    ]

Winneshiek County, Iowa, and a bank out in Nebraska. She wasn't bad looking, at the oversize stage you might say, but I don't mind these great big girls, and say, she's really a whopper." He took a sip of the brandy. Behind me the Watson girl laughed at something one of the boys with her was saying.

"Well, and you've got the farms, and the bank," I said. "What about those farms?"

"Yeah, what about those farms? In the first place it ain't three farms but one farm. In the second place it ain't 800 acres it's 100 acres. In the third place the leading crop is Russian thistle and crab grass and the farmhouse is three rooms made of rough pine and tar paper. And the fourth place, every time she gets fifty dollars off the farm she blows it on a permanent wave and a series of trips to the nearest astrologer or spirit medium. That woman of mine has blown a good small-town fortune on them rising tables. She knows more about the spirit world than she knows about the use of a frying pan, I'll guarantee that. I wish one of them spook pals of hers was to come up to the house sometime and fry me up a steak and some potatoes and leave off the six-dollar discussions of her first two husbands."

"What does she find out about the husbands, anything interesting?" I said.

"Oh hell, they're happy, or they ain't happy; they sit around there in spookland talking about the goddamnedest things. If they would give out a few hints on the stock market or who is going to cop the World Series there might be some good in it. 'Did you meet Uncle Edgar?' 'Yes,' says the spook. 'He is happy.' 'How about Cousin Lil?'

'She is happy.' Then for the daily double the table begins to jump around and some spook comes in and goes around the track a couple of times and after that everybody goes down to the lunch wagon for a red hot. How would you like to be married to a woman that was going through that performance every third day?"

"Just so she don't drink gin and sit around playing solitaire all the time," I said. "You got any kids?"

"Here leave me fill that up. On the house," he said. "I got a boy in the ladies' garment game. On the road."

"Who's the firm?"

"Futuristic Styles Inc. they call it. Owned by a couple Jews named Bernstein. Nice people. They sure treat Ben good."

"I know them," I said. "Factory in Blue Island I think."

"That's them. Me, I'd rather be dead than in selling, but why Ben, it's nothing to him. He walks right into them stores on State Street. 'Hello Myron,' he says to the buyer. 'I just come in to let you in on our new promotion. Got some dandy numbers that will fit right into your fall program.' Me, if I was to go in there my mouth would be as dry as Death Valley."

"That selling game," I said, "you either come by it natural or you might as well forget it."

"You said it there. You said it all. Me, I couldn't sell ten dollar bills for a quarter."

Marc looked down toward the door and shook his head.

"I don't know why I do it," he said. "I could work anyplace, but I gotta stay up here for some reason and put up with this climate."

Watson looked at me in the mirror and I looked at her and we both looked away and Marc said something but I wasn't listening and then I looked again and she was looking at me. Then we looked away and didn't look any more.

"Cuba, that's the place to go," Marc said. Babe came back and climbed up and sat down.

"I didn't want another drink," she said.

"Don't drink it then, baby," I said.

"Oh I guess I will," she said. She had fixed her make-up and looked better than ever.

"Cuba," Marc said. "Mr. Joyce took me down there one time in the old days. Wasn't nothing too good for us. Hotel Nacional. Say that was real air down there, 100 proof so to speak. What a spot."

When it gets to be winter out in the Middle West everything curls up and the wind begins to blow in from Saskatchewan, and the sun goes under, and even the neon lights spelling out EAT, BUDWEISER, REXALL, PACKAGE STORE, STAR BEER, STEAKS AND CHOPS begin to look cold after 5 o'clock in the evening. They roll up the windows on the city buses and the passengers crowd inside behind the fogged-up windshield. And the train whistles, which sound so passionate on a summer evening out by the new-mown hay, float and fade away as the cruel wind scatters them over the fires of the city dump and off into the night.

"Cuba, that's the place to go," Marc said.

And then when you come out of the movies in the evening, all hot with sympathy for the heroine, that stinging cold hits you and you run like hell for the drugstore on the

[    114    ]

corner, and buy a pack of cigarettes so you can wait inside until the bus comes down the street. And when you get off the bus at your stop, and step down onto the hard-packed snow, the street light is swinging to and fro, squeaking in the wind and you wonder what ever got into those guys' heads that wanted to find out what's doing at the South Pole.

"Cuba, that's the place to go," Marc said again.

"You wouldn't have to argue me into it," Babe said. "I can leave any time."

"I hear you got a strike coming up over at your place," Marc said.

"Nothing like that," I said. "Just a little dispute. Everything's gonna be O.K."

"Aha," Babe says.

"Well that's what I heard, anyways," Marc said. "Excuse me," and he went up the bar to wait on some new trade that had just come in out of the cold.

Behind us another real-life drama was going into extra innings.

"So my grandfather was a barber. All right, what if he was. The way people talk you'd think it was a crime. What if he was a barber? Tell me that. What's the matter with it? You go to the barber doncha? So does the king of England. My whole life has been just one insult after another about my grandfather and his damned barbershop."

"Aw shut up. Nobody ever knew your grandfather was a barber or what he was until you just now told us. You better sober up. Who gives a goddamn about your grandfather?"

"Listen, lay off my grandfather. I don't have to take that kinda crap off you. Just because my grandfather was a . . ."

"Oh jesus christ shut up, Roy. Just please do us a favor and shut up for a while. Will you do that? Will you just kindly oblige us for a brief period and keep your mouth shut about your grandfather?"

"There you go again. It always comes back to the same thing. I wish somebody in *your* family had been a barber and you'd see what I have to go through."

"Say, Roy, old buddy, let's have a drink, shall we kid? Come on, bozo, a good snort of Old Sunnybrook is what you need."

"Aw leave him alone, Verne. Let's get outa here and go over to the Circle and see the floor show."

"O.K. Come on, Roy."

"If you guys hadda put up with half what I do you wouldn't stand for it. No you wouldn't stand for it for ten minutes. Not for five minutes."

"Oh come on, grandpa. We're going over to the barber college to date up a couple of live wire co-eds. Pick your hat up off the floor. Come on, Roy, we've had enough of that hair-tonic routine for tonight."

Babe and I left.

So once again we paid the toll and drove across the long bridge that arched high above the frozen Mississippi. It had turned cold as hell, and the lights of the town snapped and twinkled. Would she or wouldn't she? Now was the critical moment so long awaited among the French fries, high-balls, and accordion music.

I turned off the bridge at the Iowa end and headed up through town.

"Come on up to my place for a while," I said.

She said nothing but squeezed my arm at least.

"Shall we?" I said.

"I'm sorry," she said, "but I don't want to do it like that."

"Come on, darling," I said. "Just for a while. I'll be good."

"The hell you will," she said.

"Yes I will."

"No you won't. And I wouldn't want you to be if I came up. But I'm not coming up."

"Oh hell."

"Oh hell yourself."

"All right," I said. "I don't want it like that either. But we might be dead tomorrow."

"Don't make it tough, Sid," she said. "Just take me home." She kissed me on the cheek. "I won't be dead tomorrow," she said.

Then we held hands and I drove her home.

When we got to her house up on the hill above the railroad yards I parked the car and we fell into a fearful embrace.

"We've talked about everything on God's earth," I said. "Except the main thing. Now it's time to talk about it."

"Poor Sidney," she said. "What's the matter, baby?"

"I love you, kid," I said.

*I got along finely with most Eastern boys, only
they did not understand me or my ways.*

— WILLIAM S. HART

# 13

THIS BOY Harry Kosciuszko, this friend of mine
who painted in the modern style and hung around the Art
Institute all the time, was probably the funniest painter,
possibly the only funny painter that they had over there. I
know because I used to meet Harry up there lots of times
and we would eat in the cafeteria and I got to know a lot

of the gang and go to parties and cocktail rodeos — take in
the lectures and all the exhibitions — learned the art lingo
and who was "derivative" and who had "color sense" and
why the instructors didn't like Dali ("Because he's got a
——ing sense of humor," Kosciuszko said, "and because he
can paint so goddamn good.") and who Kuniyoshi was
married to and what Pablo said to Gertrude Stein and all
the rest of it.

Here is a letter I got from Kosciuszko the day after my
argumentative date with Babe:

DEAR LITTLE VANYA:

I received the pair of pajamas you sent me for my name
day and they are very nice indeed. The sizing seems a
little bit shy but maybe I am putting on weight as a result of increasing fame and good fortune. The latest Fame
consists of a Third Prize ($50.00 cash which lasted me
forty-five minutes) in the Minneapolis show, and an
offer to teach "Art" in a college somewhere near Sapulpa
Oklahoma.

I have been worrying about you since last I saw you.
That's a hell of a cold shower to jump from Greater Chicago to some wind-swept rural community in Edgar Guest
land. What the hell do you do in the evenings? The redhead? Hell you can't go out with Red every night. But
then, I have never been able to understand what our
Vanya was doing with Potash and Perlmutter anyway.

There's a big riot scheduled for Sunday. Georgie is
leaving to teach at Colorado (an attractive deal, incidentally). Boguniesky and Santos and Mueller and Dot-
tie and the irrepressible Rothstein and of course Irene and
Renee and Levin and Whiteside and Shirley of the big

[    119    ]

tits, and Sonia of the little tits, and even repulsive Miss Winston will all be partly visible at the party. So get the lead out of your Beinkleider and step boldly up to ticket agent and we will see you Sunday. Bring Red along and give her a look at the high buildings.

Incidentally, to increase my income I have decided to use the pajamas you sent me as a sample line and invade the State Street stores. Please advise commission as I have already sold Field's, Carson-Pirie, The Fair, Finchley, etc. several rather large orders. I have developed an unusual selling technique which you might pass on to your Mr. Sales Manager. When I hit Mr. Prospect with my Sleep Tite line (the Pajama for Men of Peculiar Bedroom Habits) I usually take along with me two boys from some local football squad. (At present I am working with a tackle from New Trier High and a sophomore backfield sensation from Northwestern.) Then if Mr. Prospect says he "is overloaded already" or "will see me on my next trip" or "is waiting to see what the market will do," why football ace #1 quickly steps behind Mr. P. and applies a bar-arm, while #2 tramps on his toes and works him over with a three-foot length of garden hose. I have gotten several nice orders this way and will be glad to address the Sleep Tite salesmen at your next pep session.

I am painting a new number which will no doubt capture the pennant at the Carnegie International and I want you to come over and name it for me.

Meanwhile Julie sends greetings and we will see you Sunday and I remain,

SNOWBALL

So I wrote and told him it was all off on me coming over for the party on account of impending strike, trouble

[    120    ]

with redhead, trouble with management, trouble with workers, loss of compression, sticky valves and dishpan hands. Harry knew what that was all about because one time when he gave up art temporarily, due to starvation, I got him a job at Regal Pants where he waited on house customers and made himself generally useful and he always used to say, "You know, Sid, Al Greiner's the boy around here I feel sorry for. A superintendent for you! The poor klunk is always in the middle, gettin hell from the management on one side and from the union on the other. Hasn't got a friend in sight except Miss Friedman in the payroll office, who is hoping he will take her to the movies some night. That's some swell squeeze, a superintendent's job. And the big laugh on the deal is, the job don't pay any good anyway."

I was sitting in the office the day after that date with Babe; I was mulling it all over and wondering what was going to bust loose next. It was about ten o'clock in the morning and anyone who thinks I was feeling good after what I had gone through the night before is wrong because I was not feeling gay by a long shot — I was feeling tough.

Mr. Hines, the time-study man, came into the office and he was mighty agitated.

"I've been through a lot of troubles in my time in the industrial world," he said, "but I have never been up against anything like this."

"Mr. Hines you worry too much," I said. "What's the trouble?"

"Maybe I do worry too much," he said. "But it's plain as

the nose on your face we got a slowdown on our hands. They are . . ."

"Worry is the time-study man's occupational disease," I said. "I know all about the slowdown. What do you suggest?"

"Maybe I'm out of turn on this," he said, sitting down and nervously clicking his stop watch on and off and studying it, "but it's time for a crack-down. A few heads should roll and we'd see a different attitude here."

That line about "heads should roll" he got out of *Business Forum Monthly* — the lead article, for October, because I had read it too.

"According to contract we'd have a tough time firing anybody, even if we wanted to," I said.

Harry Kosciuszko's letter was still in front of me and there was a P.S. I hadn't seen before, to wit:

"P.S. Don't let them pull your teeth, kid," it said.

"Something could be done, I'm sure," says Time Study. "I suggest a conference with Mr. Hasler."

"A swell idea," I said. "I'll set that up right away for this afternoon."

"Trouble, trouble," said Mabel to her handy comptometer.

"Act I Scene II, *Macbeth*," I said.

"If possible I'd like to sit in on that meeting. Merely as an interested party," Mr. Hines said, getting up.

"Sure," I said. "I think it's a good idea and I'll let you know."

"Something has got to be done to bring this intolerable situation to a rapid conclusion," he said.

"I agree with you 100 per cent," I said.

"Acme steel had a case like this I was reading about in *Modern Industry* last week. They used a rather novel method of quashing the slowdown. They devised a bonus plan based on one per cent of the expected man-hour output per machine potential over a specified base of 20 per cent of the production units of average normal incentive ratio. They are getting good results and production figures show a . . ."

"That's what we need here," I said. "An incentive ratio and a good five-cent cigar. Also a 7½-cent raise and a new superintendent."

"I know how you feel," Mr. Hines said, removing and polishing his glasses. "Labor relations is one of the most complicated features that top management is faced with in the modern industrial world of the present day. It's a problem demanding . . ."

By now those twin breakfast eggs that had seemed so lovely at 7:30 A.M. at the Erie Lunch where I ate breakfast were beginning to turn slowly to lye somewhere in my midsection.

"We don't have to go into the history of the labor movement," I said, feeling very irritated with Hines and his clinical approach to every little thing. "Whatever happens, it's all Mr. Hasler's responsibility. They can't pin it on you or me or Mabel or the elevator boy, anyway."

"You know what Gantt says," he replied. "Gantt says when he is discussing autocratic control in industry as opposed to fact or organizational control, he says, 'Actions based on opinions will lose in competition with actions based on facts.'"

"Wow, he should have been in the needle trades — how unhappy he'd of been, watching his rule getting busted about ten thousand times a week," I said. "Who's Gantt, anyway, is he with the Cleveland Indians?"

"You like a good joke, I see. I think that's a good trait in management," he said.

"Yes I have a rare sense of humor," I said. "Well, who was Gantt, anyway, wasn't he one of Taylor's buddies?"

"That's right. Taylor was the Father of Scientific Management and Henry Lawrence Gantt was one of his associates. Only Gantt also believed in the human equation, he claimed that 'the era of force must give way to that of knowledge.'"

"Hines where do you get all this dope, anyway? Why with your line of jive you ought to be one of the directors of United States Steel in just a few years. You're wasting your time with that stop watch."

"Oh I've got my plans," he said. "I'm young yet."

"Listen, go out and check that rate on Liz Schreiber, will you? She's got a beef on that rate for sewing elastic."

"That woman," he said. "No concept whatsoever of the meaning of Methods Improvement. O.K., I'll check her again." He got up to go.

"I wonder," I said, "if Mr. Hasler has ever read the works of our friends Mr. Taylor and Mr. Henry Lawrence Gantt."

"I very much doubt — I'd be willing to wager — that he has never heard of them," he said.

"Is that important, I wonder," I said.

"Maybe not," he said.

"Maybe Hasler does better on instinct," I said, "than he would if he played by the scientific rules."

"Only for a while. Then always comes the explosion." He went out.

Mabel, who had been sitting there listening to us as she worked the comptometer, moving her lips, got up and came over and gave me a letter.

"At last here's that letter from Greenberg we've been waiting on," she said. "And incidentally you don't mind my saying it you don't look so good this morning in fact you look like death warmed over."

"Let's see the letter."

"Where was you last night anyways? That girl must been runnin you quite a chase."

"What's the letter say?"

The letter was from Greenberg and Aronson in Chicago as follows:

DEAR MR. SOROKIN:

Upon my return back into Chicago on arrival I immediately checked into the matter of the clutch we discussed you as definitely needing replacement on Class 71–32 Singer buttonhole. Now whereas part in question which we are shipping is not a bonified Singer part we still feel convinced you will receive satisfaction from the use of this part for your purpose. We are . . .

"The clutch they are sending ain't bonified," I said.

"So I seen from the letter," Mabel said. "Not having been up all night my eyes are in good shape — I can still read. What's that 'bonified' mean, is that bad?"

"I guess it's all right. Greenberg's steno probably ain't a bonified steno either."

"Well we're getting the part, anyway," Mabel said. "It's sure been a long wait."

"Get me the machine file, please," I said. "I want to browse through the special machines a bit." I had had a card index set up for the machine records. Every machine had a separate card with its whole medical history on it. Before that the machine records were scribbled in an old composition book with the pages all falling out. One of the big jobs then was sticking the pages together again with scotch tape once a month. My introduction of the card index caused a lot of head shaking and grumbling among the factory office staff. This was "scientific management," in an obviously dangerous form. "We never done it like that. We always kept the machine records in the machine-record book." "But this is a better way." "We never done it like that." "But this is easier, simpler, and more practical." "This book here, see, we always kept the machine records in this here book."

I thumbed through the cards on the special machines, checking dates and serial numbers and types. I get a kick out of the machines. I know a little bit about them and they are all old pals, from the old 31-15's and 61's and the 71400's and the old cylinder machines right up to the latest self-oiling 241's and the new high-speed sergers everybody is talking about.

"The production is way off," Mabel said. She had a mirror and tweezers out and was about to yank something or other off her face. Women.

"I know it," I said.

"Babe Williams is ringleadin the whole thing on fourth." Yank! "She's behind it." Yank!

"I know that too," I said.

"All right then," she put the mirror and tweezers away.

The machinist came in and sprawled in a chair under the blow-up photograph of the 1914 company picnic at Riverside Gardens.

"Well, George Hunter is gone," he said to Mabel.

"Was you to the funeral home yet?" she asked.

"I was up last night."

"I'm going tonight after supper. Who was there? Was Bud and Emily there? Or Clarence? Was any of the Ganzenmillers there?"

"I never seen nobody except that Buck Schroeder from over at Council Hill. Trust *him* to show up."

"Is he the one that run off to Muscatine with some young girl?"

"That's him. Big slob of a guy. Don't know what no young girl could of saw in him."

"How did George look?"

"Why he looked pretty good considering what he been through. He din't look so bad."

"What suit they got him in, the gray?"

"No, it was a brown suit."

"The gray was his new suit. I wonder whose idea *that* was not to lay him out in his new suit. Why that brown suit he's had that five or six years. Emily's idea I'll bet. Bud will probly show up at the Methodist church next week in the gray, wait and see."

"Well, poor old George."

"He's better off, I guess."

"He was just a burden to himself and family, it's better this way."

"I sure hope I don't go that way."

"Oh oh. Me neither."

"They say he din't eat sence last Wednesday."

"I heard his color was terrible. All chalky like and kinda greenish."

"It's a blessing to the family."

"I'll say. I guess they been through hell."

"And him how long now was he like that? Two years wasn't it?"

"Two years and four months. He left here in July I remember."

"He hardly knew me last time I seen him."

"He's better off."

"A blessing to the family."

"George was a wonderful man."

"He always treated me O.K."

"Except of course that terrible temper."

"George had a mean streak in him though."

"Are you telling *me*?"

"And then what he done to poor old Mrs. Hegan."

"The least said about that the better. Leave the dead lie in peace."

"I guess so."

"Was Verna Mae there?"

"No. All I seen was this fat slob from Council Hill. I'd

sure like to see the girl that run away with him. She couldn't be much."

"Well, I'm going up tonight."

The machinist's call rang out over the factory bell system.

"More grief," he said, and got up and went out.

"What's the news on Riordan this morning? Think she's really pregnant?" I said to Mabel.

"It don't show yet, but she took another of them dizzy spells and had to set down for fifteen minutes. She could be and then again maybe she's not."

"Hear any more about 7½ cents?"

"Plenty. And listen the bakery man didn't leave no doughnuts so I imagine we'll have a riot at lunchtime."

"Send one of the payroll girls over to the grocery store for some. What about 7½ cents?"

"Bessie Schwartz was blabbing it all over the bus this morning she says it is 7½ cents or a nice big strike, she says. 'Put that in your pipe and smoke it, Hasler, my big high-society friend,' she says. 'Bessie Schwartz,' I says to her, 'it's a crime and a shame to hear you talking that way about Mr. Hasler.' "

The elevator boy came in and tossed a pile of invoices from the accounting department on my desk to be O.K.'d.

"Is Bessie related to the big Schwartzes uptown?" I said.

"Bessie? I should say not! My god no. She comes from over in the woods someplace in Wisconsin. Why her folks run a little general store over near Big Patch. Her brother is brakeman on the Burlington . . ."

"All right," I said, trying to focus on the invoices. "I

[     129     ]

guess she's not related to the Schwartzes and we're in for a nice big strike. Merry Christmas."

"Well, you can hardly blame the help. The contract was supposed to come up in August and here it is nearly Halloween already and Mr. Hasler is still giving them the runaround."

"Mr. Hasler thinks wages are going down. Mr. Hasler has been sure wages were going down every week since he started here for six bucks a week in 1912. This time he's positive."

"My wages better not go down. I paid 78 cents for a pound of bacon yesterday for Bert. I can get along without no bacon but Bert he more than storms around if I don't give him his bacon every morning. He says . . ."

"O.K. on the bacon," I said. "Aside from the strike, how's Bert's tooth?"

"Oh my god last week he went to Dr. Baumer and what do they find but a zist on the gooms? He couldn't hardly eat no Sunday dinner. A nice goose I had, too."

"Zist on the gooms? What in hell is that?" I said. Bert had one damn thing after another. Bert was Mabel's husband and he worked at one of the mills — laid off most of the time. I got the impression he wasn't one of their favorite employees.

"Was you out with Babe last night? She must of kept you out plenty late. You better look out, or Riordan won't be the only one!"

"We had a nice uplifting evening at Bible Study."

"I'll bet you did. What church does Babe go to, then?"

"The Second Presbyterian, smarty."

[ 130 ]

"Oh, up by the coalyard. I know that church. Went to a wedding there once upon a time. Bet I'll be going to another before too very long."

"Boy you can't beat the small town," I said. "Every time you take a girl out they got you married to her. Now just forget about that, I'm not in any mood to marry anybody. It's a wonder they don't talk about you and me because we sit here alone in this office all day."

"Don't think it ain't been mentioned," she said, and laughed.

"That's all," I said. "Never mind the rest. I'll go out and make the rounds of the plant and see how the nice big strike is developing."

I ran into Mr. Hines, with his stop watch and board, heading for his office.

"What about Liz Schreiber?" I said. "Get her cooled down yet?"

"No, I wouldn't say so. I must say the modern psychological approach just breaks down completely when applied to this Schreiber woman."

"Want me to talk to her?" I said.

"Don't think you'll get very far," he said. "She's off on one of her rampages. I wish sometimes top management could know what we go through out here on the firing line."

"Liz likes to kick and scream once in a while. It makes her feel important."

"I know," he said. "And by the way, how about coming to Associated Foremen tomorrow night? Good speaker from National Screw Products in Toledo. He's going to give us

[    131    ]

a talk on 'Are Your Foremen Part of the Management Team?' Wish you'd come up some time. Sure you'd find it worth while."

One of the foreladies rushed up to me.

"Them buttons didn't come in yet and we're holding up the whole lot. I'm sure I don't know why they can't seem to get the buttons to us on time. And the thread on 25X don't match. Oh I don't know why I ever give up sewing to take this job. I got half a notion to give the whole thing up. I can make more money on a machine anyhow. Why I use to make $1.10 an hour on piece rates when I was a pocket setter. I was the fastest operator in . . ."

"Now listen, Pearl," I said. "You like being a forelady and you know it! Why, you're on the management team."

"Some team," she said. "Where are the buttons, that's all I want, them buttons. Them high and mighty ones in Supplies are too busy smoking cigarettes, I suppose, to bother about a thing like that."

"I'll see if I can dig up a sub," I said. "And never mind about the thread match. It won't show on those garments."

"All right," she said. "And tell that kid they got on the elevator that the next time he stops to talk to Helen Baumgarden he'll find himself at the bottom of the elevator shaft."

"O.K.," I said. "I'll tell him." And I went to see Liz Schreiber.

"What's the trouble?" I said.

"Trouble, why your wonderful Hines set a rate on this here elastic job so low that Jesus Christ himself couldn't make 90 cents an hour on them. He's a sneaky shifty rat,

[    132    ]

that's what I think of the great Mr. Hines and I told him so myself. Took me an hour and a quarter to get out my last bundle. Goddamn it if it isn't a crime and a shame what I put up with around this dump."

The setting of rates and the reaction by the operators is a routine you have to go over again and again, forever and ever, apparently, as long as there shall be garment plants, superintendents, sewing-machine operators, piece rates, and broken needles. You study carefully and set the rate, say 49½ cents a dozen for hemming. You post the rate and then the operator has a fit. She says she can't make nothing on that rate. She says she's been here on the line for twenty-three years and no young squirt time-study man is going to push her around. You tell her there's a lot of factors involved (what would we do without those involved factors?), and that management wants to meet the operators half way and continue to enjoy mutual confidence for the highest production, Sleep Tite quality, and high earnings based on output and ability. The operator says she can't buy no groceries on mutual confidence and is going to go work at the Packing Plant unless something is done about that rate. The other girls in the unit glare at Management and exchange significant looks and talk so much about it all day that production goes off twelve dozen. You promise to analyze the situation and make an "eight-hour study" to check for any factors that might have been overlooked (or involved).

Next day the time-study man takes an all-day study and finds that he forgot to allow one-half minute per hour for "grasp scissors with left hand, clip estimated two threads per dozen, return and release scissors to position on machine table," and this raises the rate .0015 per doz.

You announce this raise to the operator and she invokes the Sherman Anti-Trust Laws and the Emancipation Proclamation and says she is being crucified.

Then there is a formal protest by the Union President. You hold a meeting in the private office. "Mutual confidence" is mentioned.

The operator says she can't eat mutual confidence and that she can't make even 75 cents an hour on that rate, and she been here on the line twenty-three years.

You agree to raise the rate from 49½ cents per doz. to 50¼ cents. Two weeks later the operator is running away with the rate and making $1.33 an hour, within 17 cents of the machinist, who is the best machinist in the area and knows more about a Singer machine than the Singer people.

(Sometimes you refuse flatly to raise the rate but it is understood according to the unwritten rules of this peculiarly formalized game, that the fun is over now and the jabber is at an end. Whether there is a little adjustment made or not, after this last conference the operator goes back to work and quits wasting time squawking. It's been a nice break in the monotony and the operator has played it for all it was worth and squeezed the part dry. Now let's get to work again!)

"Listen, Liz," I said. "Do me a personal favor and try the rate until the first of the year. Just try it and see how it works out. Will you do that?"

"And we ain't even heard a word about the contract, neither," she said.

[    134    ]

"Will you try the rate? An operator like you, twenty-three years in here, why there's nothing to hold you back on a Singer machine. Let yourself go. Show us what you can do."

"I can walk out, that's what I can do," she said, but she was feeling better from having shot her wad, and about ready to go to work.

"All right," she said. "I'll try it. Good thing you got some old fools like me around this place."

"Good girl," I said. "Listen, Hines is not so bad as you think. He's been mighty worried about your problem here. That's why he's checked it three times. We wanna be *sure* that one of our best operators is getting every possible break."

"Soft soap," she said. "You must buy it by the barrel."

"You just pack up your troubles about the rate," I said. "Just forget about the rate — and warm up this old Singer. You're gonna surprise yourself."

"I'll bet," she said. "Anyway, somebody around this plant is gonna get some surprises soon."

"I don't like that kinda talk," I said.

"I bet you don't," she said.

*A Western Union Collect* BARABOO WIS
700 P M — WHERE IN THE HELLO ARE MY
SAMPLES HAVE BEEN WAITING HERE FOR
THEM THREE DAYS ADVISE

— CASEY

# *14*

I WENT UP to the fourth floor of the plant and I
stood by one of the large dirty windows and looked out over
the town to the east. Right below me were the tops of the
little red-brick rooming houses and grocery stores and
taverns, with dirty snow on the roofs and along the streets
old ladies walked carefully in their black coats with brown

[ 136 ]

imitation-fur collars, clutching loaves of bread, ham sausage, wieners, and heads of cabbage. Beyond was Grand Avenue, filled with trucks and semitrailers, some from the John Deere plant leaving town loaded with bright shiny green tractors that looked like Christmas toys from a distance, some coming in from the west with hogs bound for the last rites at the packing house, and some from the east: transports with automobiles from Detroit miraculously nested together and balancing as they filled the street with their magic shine.

Beyond Grand Avenue and the traffic and the old ladies with their string bags, the Watson Pump Works stood in majestic bulk as it would do until Eternity. So big and proud a mountain of brick and stone that it would endure, obviously, forever.

# WATSON – SINCE 1872

it said to the world on the very top of the biggest pump works in this or any other world.

To the east of Watson — Since 1872 was the Mississippi River. Over in Illinois, small and remote, were the roofs, insignificant in the daytime, of the bars in which all problems were solved in the late evenings, when the factories grew dark and the lights across the river beckoned to disconnected citizens to come and play and have French frieds, accordion music, and sloe gin fizzes, and forget the gas bill, telephone bill, and grocery bill.

And beyond the taverns were the hills of Illinois, rising to the prairie, with Chicago two hundred miles away: State

[    137    ]

Street, Madison Street, the Els and the dirt in alleys and the Palmer House — Union Station, the Lake, the cold sting, bellhops, overheated hotel rooms, the cast-iron filigree above Carson Pirie's entrance. And me over in Iowa with Watson — Since 1872. And Hasler. And 7½ cents.

The soot rained down and in the alley below me, a kid was trying for some fun on his sled among the garbage cans and parked trucks.

It was funny but Babe's part in the thing didn't make me a damn bit mad. She was labor and I was Capital with a big C now and she was doing what I'd have done and what I was perfectly at ease to see her doing in this divine mess.

Behind me a couple of operators were jabbering away above the hum and whirr and buzz of their high-speed Singers — always blabbing all the time, my god how the people in this town kept the jaws flapping:

"Well, Myrna's baby died!" screams one, feeding elastic into the automatic short-length cutter.

"Pre-matoor, wasn't it?" screams the other.

"No, I din't hear that."

"I heard it was pre-matoor."

"It was only five months."

"Yeah, I heard it was pre-matoor."

"No, five months."

Life, as the man says, is funny. One day you are in Gary High School practicing clarinet cadenzas for the orchestra and trying to get a date for the dance with Marie Kowalski of the beautiful dark eyes, and the next thing you know difficulties than those involving boilers and buttonholes. The Union is about to strike for a 7½ cents wage increase, and there he is, between Babe, his redhead tornado, on the one hand, and Mr. Hasler, his boss, on the other. Mr. Hasler has been sure wages were going down every week since he started at the shop for six bucks a week in 1912. Now he's positive.

It's a funny book, but not all farce. There is an undertone of seriousness that gives it character, and a note—in spite of torrid bedroom scenes—of true romance. *So then I kissed her and the angels gathered on the sidewalk beside us and sang songs and played on their mouth organs.*

The people at Sleep Tite play poker and drink beer and gossip. The young make love in a bold, sure way quite unknown to a Henry James character, with a vocabulary no screen hero could ever indulge in. The book might have been a comic or a social document. But it is neither. As it stands it is a familiar corner of American life. 7½ CENTS won't be the most refined book on your shelf, but it will be taken off the shelf oftener than most books, and it will be read.

BOOK-OF-THE-MONTH CLUB, INC.
*345 Hudson Street, New York 14, N. Y.*

ain't got steam?

On the fourth floor are the girls, sewing by hand and machine, among them two or three queens (Sid Sorokin speaking). Delores Paradiso is one of the queens, a quiet brunette with olive skin and enormous dark eyes, who puts buttonholes in the flys of men's pajamas with a genteel air as though she were pouring tea at the Junior League. Babe Williams is another, a nice healthy-looking redhead whom Sorokin has his eye on. Babe operates a Union Special 51400 and can set more sleeves in an 8-hour day than any operator between Omaha and Fort Wayne.

In the office, working directly with Mr. Hasler and Sid, is Mabel. Mabel is about 43 or 48 or 51, a big energetic girl who has the goods on every operator, every cutter and even the elevator boy, back to the first generation, including out-of-town connections and relations on the other side of the family.

*"Who's dead now?"* asks Sid.

*"Old Mrs. Schilsky. You wouldn't know her. You should of seen the flowers."*

*"Who's old Mrs. Schilsky?"*

*"Well, I never knew her but her son married a girl that used to live next door to us in Cuba City when I was in grade school. . . ."*

This then is the setup at Sleep Tite. What is doesn't take Sid long to find out is that there are greater

Richard Bissell is not poking fun at them. He is having a wonderful time with them, and like his hero, Sid Sorokin, he is irrepressible. It seems more than likely that he too has worked in a pajama factory.

This particular factory is in a place Mr. Bissell calls Junction City, Iowa, right across the river from Illinois. It makes Sleep Tite, the Pajama for Men of Bedroom Discrimination. The man who runs it is Myron Hasler, who dotes on Fulton Lewis, Jr., and at whose approach every knot of workers dissolves. When Mr. Hasler looks at you, says Sid Sorokin, you want to hide behind the wastepaper basket.

Sid is the young new superintendent in charge of the plant, fresh out of a cutting room in Chicago. Under him are some 500 girls on pants and buttons and sleeves and collars, besides assorted help.

The elevator boy at Sleep Tite quit school because he wasn't getting noplace there and now sits on a wooden machine box getting someplace reading the funnies.

Down in the boiler room the steam fitters are cussing the boiler. There ought to be a new boiler, says Sid. The boiler is like new, says Mr. Hasler. It was put in the day after President Harding was killed, says Mabel, and that's not old for a boiler.

Up on the second floor are the pressers waiting for steam. First we got steam all over the place and no pajamas coming down the chutes, says the beefy forelady. Then we got pajamas up to the ceiling all at once and we got no steam. What do I know why we

A NOVEL BY
*Richard
Bissell*

# 7½ Cents

A REPORT BY *Bernardine Kielty*

*Reprinted from the Book-of-the-Month Club News*

THIS NOVEL about a pajama factory is a funny novel, funny because it is familiar. Most of us will feel right at home among these garrulous good-natured fellow citizens of ours. Their talk is around us everywhere—like the mayonnaise in diner sandwiches. Their pleasures, strictly at the juke-box level, we share on the air. Their humor is born of comics.

you're standing over in a foreign state looking out a window at some crummy old pump factory.

First you want to be a virtuoso in the woodwinds and the old man, born in Kiev, and the mamushka, born in Odessa, think it is great and the old man plays duets with you, him with his violin, and pays for a good teacher out of his wages at the Steel Mill and brags you up over the vodka with his friends. Then you grow up and you decide to be an American Hero and get a big car and a tuxedo and a house with overstuffed furniture, so you leave the clarinet to gather dust on top of the old upright piano and you go to work in the Regal Pants Inc., spreading piece goods for Shapiro. You give mamushka six dollars a week but the old man is mad and won't play duets any more.

You spread enough cloth for Shapiro to put two pairs of pants on everybody in America and then Shapiro teaches you how to mark and you are a marker and buy a new suit for $19.50 at Richman Brothers on State Street and give the mamushka nine dollars every week but the old man is still mad and won't play duets.

You mark pants and you go to night school and learn Patterns and Grading and ride home late at night on the South Shore train studying the hockey scores in the tabloid and when you walk home from the station to the flat where the clarinet is gathering dust on top of the upright piano your shoes make squeaky metallic noises in the hard packed snow.

Shapiro makes you a cutter and so you are a cutter and you study more books and go to more night school and take Labor Relations and Business Law and the History of Everything. You give mamushka twelve dollars a week and buy the kid sister a tortoise-shell toilet set for her birthday and Harry Kosciuszko introduces you to the Art Institute gang and you buy a five-dollar shirt and shine your shoes and you study and push and Shapiro loves you but the old man still is mad, because he wanted you to be a virtuoso clarinet with the Chicago Civic Orchestra instead of in the garment trade, so he won't play duets any more, even when you get the clarinet down off the upright piano and dust it off and run some scales and play the clarinet part from Tchaikovsky's Fourth.

Shapiro gives you a raise and the Designer dies and Shapiro is going to give you a whack at the job — with all your night school you can do pattern work and grade patterns by now. So you take Marie Kowalski out and you kiss her under a street light two blocks from the railroad tracks and then the next evening at the Union Meeting they elect you Treasurer of the Local on account of all the night school and brains. So now Shapiro is mad at you because you are a union officer and he figures you have double-crossed him, but after supper the old man takes down his violin case and begins to tune the fiddle and the kid sister gets going on the upright piano and you play some duets with piano accompaniment and the mamushka is happy and brings out the brandy and two glasses, for father and son, big musicians and union men.

Shapiro is not playing any duets with you any more but you get an increase and you go to more night school and take Elementary Time Study, Standard Data, and the History of Europe since 1815, and you buy a gray-flannel

suit wholesale from Hart Schaffner and Marx. You have
a brief but terrible love affair with one of Harry's art
student friends. With her in her bangles and blouses and
ballerina shoes, you go to the theater and have late suppers at unclean upstairs Italian restaurants and afterwards on the South Shore train you study the late baseball
scores in the tabloid.

By now you have been to nine years of night school and
there is hardly anything you don't know but you sign up
for Personnel Problems, Advanced Labor Relations, Quality
Control, and Fine Arts of the Renaissance. Then you are
sitting in the kitchen reading the paper and drinking coffee
and the kid sister is playing Chaminade on the upright and
there is this ad in the classified ads that says under HELP
WANTED, MALE:

> Superintendent — garment plant making mens pajamas.
> 200 machines. 200 miles from Chicago in town of 50,000.
> Unusual opportunity for qualified man. Write CX501.

Then a few days later you are in room 1452 at the
Stevens and out the window the lake is ever so blue and
you wonder what ever possessed you to answer that ad.
There's a tall skinny old boy there with a bald head and he
gives you a cigarette and you are so balled up you don't say
hardly a thing but in a few days you get a letter from the
state of Iowa and it says you are hired so you buy a suit-
case as this is the first time you have ever been out of town
and you leave the old clarinet on top of the piano and go.
You get on a Burlington train and read the *Daily News*
for three hours and then you are getting off the train and

according to instructions you get into a bus. The bus rambles down a wide street with nothing but saloons, and takes a right turn and you are on a big bridge.

"That's the Mississippi River," says a soldier sitting behind you.

"So what?" says another soldier. "Last week it was the Sacramento. So what?"

Now I stood there looking down over the town and thinking of all this and wondering whether I was making a fool of myself. There was Hasler and all that, and Babe and all that, and Mabel and 7½ cents and Mr. Hines with his quotations from Gantt, and Bernstein was coming from Chicago.

Down in the alley below me the kid had managed to knock over a garbage can and the contents was strewn on the dirty crust of the snow. A witch came out on a sagging porch and screamed at him.

Back in the office Sam Dolinoff was waiting for me. Sam was a used sewing machine buyer. He was a heavyset guy about fifty in a d. b. hard-finish worsted in a new shade of blue.

"How are ya, Sid?" he said. "Long time no see. Congrats on the new job."

"Hello Sam," I said. "How's it over in Chicago?"

"Here, smoke this," he said giving me a cigar.

"I haven't smoked a cigar since I was twelve years old," I said. "Here, Mabel, you give this to Bert, I'll bet he smokes cigars."

"Listen kid, you want a Deepfreeze?" Sam said. "I got a new hookup. I can get you a hundred bucks off the list."

"I live in a furnished two-room flat," I said. "What would I keep in a Deepfreeze, my tennis racket and old shoes? All I need is some peace and quiet. And try and get some in a garment plant."

"All right, all right, so you don't want a Deepfreeze. But listen, any time you want anything, let me know — radio, refrigerator, nice latest model gas stoves, all national brands — sure, I can get you what you want. Leave me know. Just give me a buzz any time. Have a Ford for you in forty-eight hours. Any paint job you want. Easy. Want a good vacuum cleaner for your old lady's birthday? You name the make — any make. Thirty bucks off the list."

"Sam, believe me — and stop dragging on that cigar so hard, you'll burn the place down — believe me, I don't want a thing, either at list or under list. I got a car, a wrist watch, six suits of clothes — I'm all set, pal. Forget it, will you?"

"Where you get your suits? Jack Goldman, over at Hart Schaffner, and I are like this. Any time. Just give me a buzz when you're in town. Take you right over myself."

"I get my suits at Moe's Emporium in Blue Island. I got too many suits anyway."

"Look at this suit," he said. "Nice drape, huh? How much you think? Feel the goods."

"Twenty-two fifty," I said. "What the hell do you want? You're driving me crazy."

"Sid, ain't you got a few machines laying around I can make a few bucks on? Sure, boy, you got some stuff for Sammy. How about it?"

"I got about twenty-five old 61's. For ten bucks apiece they're yours."

"I don't want no 61's and neither does nobody else. I'll give you four dollars apiece."

"So long, Sam, that's all I got."

"How about that overedge machine you said you was going to get rid of?" says Mabel, determined to get in the conversation and getting in at just the wrong time.

"Mabel, you're a swell girl," I said, "and I love you. But will you please get going on those cutting tickets?"

"Well," she says, "you said only Friday you was going to get a new one when that Willcox and Gibbs man was here."

"Where is it at?" says Sam, getting up and going to the door of the office. "Leave me see it, Sid. I'll take it right with me in the car. Save you the packing and shipping."

"I'm saving it for a trade-in," I said. "And I might need it yet anyway. I didn't decide to sell it yet. I didn't decide yet what to do with that machine."

"Leave me have a look at it. Cash on the line. Then you won't have to worry no more about that old machine one way or another."

"I don't wanna sell it, Sam," I said.

"What is it, Singer or Willcox? 81–2? What's the serial number?"

"It's in the shop on the bench. Go and look at it if it'll make you any happier."

He went out to the shop and I opened the window to let some of the smoke out.

[    144    ]

"He pays good prices sometimes," Mabel said. "Why don't you wanna sell it to him?"

"Mabel, for heaven's sake, I'm *going* to sell it to him. Just let me work with Sammy without any inside instructions, will you please?"

"Well you don't ack like you was going to. How could I tell?"

"Call up Bert and find out how his toothache is, why don't you?" I said.

We had this old overedge machine depreciated down to about fifteen dollars. The week before a guy had offered me thirty for it. I thought I could get forty.

"Whadda you want for it," Sam said when he came back, and lit a new cigar. He twisted the cellophane wrapper into a knot and put it in the ashtray.

"All those cigars will stunt your growth," I said. "I want forty bucks for it and I don't mean thirty, thirty-one-fifty, or thirty-eight. Forty bucks is the price and I'll get it from somebody."

"That machine must of been old man Singer's working model," he said. "It's so old the operators have wore the name off it. The needle in it seems to be a late model, so I'll give you twenty bucks if you throw in the needle."

"How's your family, Sammy?" I said. "That boy of yours on the basketball team this year?"

"Twenty-five. I got to pay for my gas and oil anyways."

"How's the Cadillac on gas?" I said. "What mileage you get on that wagon?"

"I can't make a dime on that old clunker at forty bucks.

How about it, Sid, plug up your courage and sell it to me. I can use that machine."

"I heard Benny Erlanger got the superintendent's job at New-Mode. He's a smart kid, Benny. I used to work with him at Regal."

"You want me to make a living, don't you? I'd like to make ten bucks on that old antique. Whadda you say, Sid?"

"I say forty bucks. When we were in a jam for a 175–60 machine you got one for Shapiro right quick. Remember the price? 675 dollars. There was a war on then. Now the war's over and I want forty bucks for that old beat-up over-edge machine."

He laid four tens on my desk.

"Now what else you got?" he said, and his cigar ash cascaded down the lapel of his Hart Schaffner special.

"You're gonna ruin that suit if you keep on dousing it in ashes," I said. "I haven't got any other machines, Sam, except those 61's. And they're still ten bucks apiece."

"What I could use is a buttonhole machine. Haven't you got some poor old buttonhole machine you can leave go? I'll give you two hundred for any old clunker."

"Sure, I've got two old relics, and I'm saving them for parts."

"Gimme a receipt on the machine," he said.

"I'll have the boy put it in your car," I said.

"You better ship it," he said. "I'd get the blues with that poor orphan in the car with me."

"What did you buy it for?" I said. "You know it's a lemon."

"I got to buy something, Sid — that's my business. Who knows, some schlemiel might come in next week who just gotta have that machine. Just that particular machine."

"I suppose so," I said. Outside a few idle snowflakes drifted against the office windows. "Beginning to snow again. You heading west, I suppose?"

"Royal Overall in Cedar Falls is up for sale. I'm not out here to make a million off no forty-dollar overedge machine. I'm out to buy Royal Overall. One hundred machines, all late models, on direct drive stand."

"You better get going or you'll end up with the famous Cadillac in a snowdrift and you sleeping in somebody's hayloft. We're due for a big snow."

"They don't have no snowstorms in October over here," he said, pulling on his dark-blue vicuña overcoat.

"That's what it said on the radio anyway," I said. "And when it snows over here it really snows, so they say. What do you think that white stuff on the roofs out there is?"

"None of my business, Sid, but I hear you're having labor troubles. I hear you're in for some kinda grief or another. Anything in it?"

"Where in the hell did you hear that? Did you see Rubenstein in Chicago or something?"

"No, I stopped off in Freeport at Ace Glove and Mitten. Sullivan hired one of your operators the other day. Her husband got transferred over there so she come in for a job. She told him you was havin a slowdown over here. She says to him she says, 'I'm glad I got out when I did. I don't wanna be in no strike.' That don't sound so good, Sid. What's it all about?"

"There's not gonna be any strike," I said. "But we've got one helluva swell slowdown going on."

"Didn't you give the 7½ cents increase yet?" he said.

"No and the management says we ain't going to," I said.

"I wish 'em luck with that idea," he said. "How they figure they're gonna put it over when everybody else already give the 7½ cents over a month ago, even Kelly-Schonheit, them tight-fisted kikes."

"I'm just the superintendent, don't ask me," I said.

"Personally I think these increases are crazy as hell," he said, reaching for his hat. "Pajamas are so high now that I have bought my last pair. But what can you do?"

"Fight 'em," I said. "My boss is a fighter. He's gonna make an example of them he says."

"Send me a telegram if he does," Sam said. "And I'll send him a dozen American Beauty roses."

"You better get going," I said. "Hope you get what you want in Cedar Falls."

"So do I," he said. "I ain't gonna pay my expenses with this big deal here on that overedge machine."

"So long," I said.

"Good luck on that strike," he said.

Sam left and I checked a note through to the machinist about shipping the machine I had sold.

"Want a caramel?" Mabel said, pulling a candy box out of her drawer.

"No, thanks," I said. "But you go right ahead and have one anyway."

"Was you out with Babe Williams last night?"

[    148    ]

"Yeah. I was out with Babe."

*I love you, kid.*

"I knew you was anyway because Ramona Schiltz seen you and her go into the International."

*You're out of this world, Baby.*

"Ramona Schiltz is a nice name," I said.

*And when I hold you in my arms the world's all right.*

"Her sister took to the drink and ended up in a sanitarium," Mabel replied.

*Babe I love you, darling.*

"What was her name, the sister?"

*You're so goddamn beautiful lover with that auburn hair.*

"Delores. She married into the Callahans."

*All the birds and bees do it.*

"Then she was Delores Schiltz Callahan. That's quite a mixture."

*With tender arms I crush thy form divine.*

"She got to drinking. They couldn't do nothing with her," Mabel continued.

*With this kiss I thee wed o heavenly redhead.*

"I am sorry about it," I said.

The elevator boy came into the office and laid some papers on my desk.

"This just come up from the main office," he said.

"What's been happening to Marvin Stacy, Master Sleuth lately?" I said.

"Him and Buddy the Boy Detective are after this here crook called Peahead now. This guy with a real little head."

He went out.

[    149    ]

There was a pink sheet which was used for correspondence from the salesmen, and a note pinned to it. The note
was from Hasler.

No excuse — inefficiency someplace — typical of production dept. — co-ordination lacking — I want full ex-
planation.

M. HASLER.

I read the pink sheet attached:

WRITE ON ONE SUBJECT ONLY

BE BRIEF

*To*: HASLER
*From*: MURDOCK

Out of the last lot of new pajama samples sent me last
week I don't think there were any two that had the collers
folded alike no uniformaty whatever, on samples 313 and
349 the collers looked terrible why can't you get someone
at the factory that knows how to fold a paj. like the Fullbright paj. if its the cut of our coller I think its about time
someone got on the ball and changed the pattern we have
the worse looking pajama in the field Sears Wards and
Penneys have better looking paj. collers then we do, we
have a nice antique style paj. coller if we stay with it
much longer maybe it will come back in style again. Why
don't you modernize. Who in h—— have you got in
charge there anyway I hear you have got some boy wonder now he must be a honey is all I can say some day you
will get wise as to what the paj. game is all about but
it might be to late then.

MURDOCK

"What's the matter with you?" Mabel said. "You look like you was ready to murder somebody. What's the matter?"

I got up and went over to her desk and laid it in front of her.

"Read it," I said.

"Oh my," she said as she read it. "Oh my this is terrible."

"*I* never drafted that collar pattern," I said. "*What* the hell. I knew I was nutty to take this job."

"Now don't get excited. Calm down. We get something like this every once in a while."

"Look at Hasler's note. 'Inefficiency. Co-ordination lacking. Typical of Production Dept.' That's nice ain't it?"

"Now calm down. Don't fly off the handle."

"Well what the hell," I said. "I mean what the hell anyway."

"Calm down," Mabel said.

"I'm in no mood to calm down. I don't have to take this kind of crap off anybody. I'm finished. You can measure up this desk for some other poor sap. I'm going back to Chicago," I said.

"Listen, sit down, quit talking crazy," Mabel said.

"Oh what the hell," I said. "I been in this game thirteen years." Boy was I ever fed up to the back teeth. "I don't have to take this stuff," I kept saying with monotonous insistence.

"Wait a minute," Mabel said. "Sit down and cool off. My, why you sound like Mr. Coots. Oh how he used to carry on when he would get one of them notes from Mr. Hasler. Oh he would go wild."

I began to think of Babe. Somehow I had to hang onto one thing at least in this wonderful new world I had created for myself by answering that damnable ad in the World's Greatest Newspaper.

"Coots use to get so mad, especially for an easy-going type of man," Mabel said.

*Girl of my dreams I love you.*

It wasn't working very well. I was too damn mad.

"What is this Hasler anyway?" I said. "Doesn't he know what this game adds up to? Tell me, what's the matter here anyway? Is it me?"

"Now calm down, Mr. Sorokin," Mabel said, "and I'll tell you all about it. Sit down."

"All right tell me," I said. Oh Babe, this is no place for you and me.

*You're turning night into day.*

"Listen. Mr. Hasler is no doubt a fine man and highly thought of and a Past President of the Rotary Club, but my lands, *he* don't knowing nothing about the manufacturing end of the business. Now here's a typical example I mean of the kind of stuff he pulls off around here. Now don't ever let on I told you."

She went over and closed the office door, fiddled with the strings to the Venetian blind, and sat down again at her cluttered-up desk.

"Once upon a time Belle Casey got mad at Sadie Hanson some reason. Something about the electric fans. She wanted them on and Hanson wanted them off, I don't know, some crazy stuff — anyway Casey walked out and went home.

" 'Where's that lot of samples?' Hasler says. 'We had to put another girl on the elastic machine,' I says. 'Casey walked out.' 'What'd you let her do that for?' he says. 'That's poor supervision.' I felt like telling him where to stick his 'poor supervision.' 'Why there's nothing much to do when Casey gets mad. She's gonna *go*, that's all,' I says. 'Get her back,' he says. 'Her Irish is up,' I says. 'She won't come back until tomorrow.' 'Get her on the phone,' he says, looking like Teddy Roosevelt mad about something. 'I'll talk to her,' he says. That was some conversation. She give it to him in the key of G. 'You're violating the contract,' says Hasler. She told him what to do with the contract. Finally he gave up. 'Do any good?' I says as though I hadn't of been listening. 'No,' he says. 'She took a very unco-opera-tive attitude.' 'I guess you was talking to Casey all right,' I says. 'Fire her,' he says. 'They have to realize who's run-ning this place.' 'Oh we can't do that Mr. Hasler,' I says. 'Why she's the best elastic girl we ever had in here. And she's got an old father all crippled up with the arthritis to support.' 'Oh good lord,' he says. 'And besides,' I says, 'she's union chairlady in her section.' 'Oh good Lord,' he says, 'we might as well be in Russia.' And he goes back to the main office to his big desk."

"What happened with Casey?"

"Oh, she come back in the next morning all smiles. Put out over sixty dozen that day. Now you see what I mean?"

"Yeah, I see," I said.

[ 153 ]

"Get me some stock pajamas up here," I said. "I want to see what they look like. Must be something going wrong, with the salesmen as hot as all that. What the hell's the matter down there in the finishing section — do you and I have to stand behind them with a club? What is going on? Oh that Hasler. Me for the back alleys."

Mabel popped a Tums into her mouth and came over to my desk where I was unhappily clutching this awful communiqué. Babe was so far away from me now she might as well have been on a National Geographic Society expedition.

"This Murdock," Mabel said. "Let me tell you about this salesman Murdock, he has been with the firm thirty years, and every time he runs into some account gives him the bum's rush he writes in one of these letters like you see here. Why Livingston, the star salesman, sold that big order to Carson Pirie only last week what you worrying about this thing for? You know what life on the road is like — these poor salesmen when they don't sell some big account they been counting on why they go into one terrible slump they set there in the hotel room brooding over it and after a while they go out and meet some other drummer down in the lobby and start chewing the rag about all their troubles and then they get feeling so sorry they go across the street and commence drinking beer and about three hours later they come back to the room and write the house one of these here letters how rotten the product is. Oh my goodness we been through this thing a million times. No use to take it so hard. Mr. Hasler will forget all about it in the morning."

"Hasler hasn't forgotten anything since they tried to impeach President Johnson," I said.

*If I could be with you one hour tonight.*

"You remind me of Mr. Coots," Mabel said. "The way you carry on. You want an aspirin tablet?"

"Morphine is what I need," I said.

The elevator boy came in sideways and laid a big long sealed company envelope on my desk and went out in a hurry.

"This is it," I said. "I don't think I'll even wait for sundown to leave town. I better call a cab and get outside the city limits."

"That's funny," Mabel said. "Very seldom any sealed envelopes come up here from the office. Open it up."

We looked at it. So then I opened it up:

I have it on good authority that the ringleader of the uncalled for Slow Down that is causing production loss is an operator in pants section named Catherine Williams. Get rid of Williams at once!

MYRON HASLER

*Many executives have admitted that praising usually does not occur to them, while criticizing does.*

— GETTING THINGS DONE IN BUSINESS

## 15

PERHAPS IT IS TIME, or overtime, to explain the peculiar position of a Superintendent of Plant in the garment industry, and my role as same.

Superintendents are "hired help" in all except the family type of business, where you might find some brother-in-law, or some son who can't understand a Dun report

[    156    ]

or sell the line or wrap packages, holding down the job. Most superintendents are wise guys who have come up the hard way from the cutting room, but who have out-smarted themselves by knowing so much about piece rates and seam construction and all the rest of the production mysteries that in Management's mind they have reached the peak of their usefulness. They think that someday they are going to get out of the dugout and be sent to play third-base position on the Board of Directors, but this never happens. They are just hired help like the machinist and if they get sore and want some stock why they are told that superintendents are two for a quarter and if they are unsatisfied they better look for something else. So they move over to another plant and go through it all over again until one day they are attractively displayed in the latest model casket with three handles on each side and the floral offering from the firm is viewed and dis-cussed by all the visitors and they still haven't even got one share of stock.

Now whereas the average man with one wife to put up with is often hard pressed to remain outside the laughing academy, the superintendent of a garment plant has 100 to 500 or more women on his hands in varying stages of intimacy ranging from hatred to the schoolgirl crush. In some men this can breed strange mental conflicts yet to be classified by Professor Jung. Others, such as myself, take a wild sort of pleasure in living amidst this chaos of feminine charm. In either case life is not simple compared to that of Clyde Beatty.

Bawling out somebody who is likely to burst into tears

or slump to the floor of the office in a faint, poses some interesting problems in approach. You've got to come out with it and tell them that unless they get on the ball and quit blabbing so much and get down to work that you are going to fire them. Now how to go about it without a riot? Or you have got to tell the girl who is obviously about six months along that she has got to go home and stay there. Another nice task.

Well, it is all in the game as the boys say, but the Top Management wouldn't do it for Junior Ford's salary.

In addition to this atmosphere of more or less constant tension, the superintendent, god love him, is responsible for everything connected with production: output, costs, quality, personnel, window shades, floor wax, heat, light, power, busted toilets, busted machines, busted steam lines, ice on the front steps — *everything*, the poor bastard. And, meanwhile, he is caught out in the middle between the lines of good old Labor and good old Top Management, with both sides pouring hot lead at him three times a day; he spends a lot of time dodging the minie balls and grape shot and when five o'clock comes it is quite a relief for the old boy to lie down in his tracks until tomorrow's shooting starts. And if it doesn't start up tomorrow it will later in the week. Or next week.

However, all this is part of the job, and nobody has to be a superintendent of a garment plant unless he wants to. So far I can't say I had been having a very bad time. Having a pretty *good* time as a matter of fact.

The only big trouble actually was the "lines of authority," so-called. Mr. O'Hara owned the controlling stock and was

President and General Manager. He had buyers and stylists and "Sales Engineers" (that's a good one) and credit men and all that, and he had Mr. Hasler, who was Vice-President in Charge of Production. The way this worked out was that although Hasler didn't know a Singer 241 from a 1916 Pierce-Arrow, due to never having worked a day in a garment plant, he had the last say on everything I tried to do in the plant.

"Now these new direct-drives with the individual motors, Mr. Hasler," I once said to him. "You get an immediate pickup to top speed and eliminate belt-calls. The clutch . . ."

Believe it or not, they were still running off line shafts.

"How much does it cost?" he said.

"You can increase production up to 15 per cent and reduce piece rates."

"How much does it cost?"

"They cost about 75 dollars apiece including new stand and table-top."

"With our 300 machines that's an outlay of 22,500 dollars plus freight, installation and extras."

"You can fire the belt-boy, increase production, and . . ."

"We'll wait until the others put them in."

"But all the others *have* put them in. I'll bet there's not a plant in Chicago or Milwaukee operating today off line shafts."

"Well, this isn't Chicago."

That's what I was up against, and it went all the way from marking paper to that old, inefficient, beat-up steam boiler that was costing us 50 to 100 dollars a month

[      159      ]

in steam fitters' and boilermakers' bills to hold together.

I didn't have the outright authority to buy a new broom hardly.

And in labor negotiations, I was in the same spot. I could talk and argue, and fight for the company, and use my good slavic brains, and try to beat the union, but when it came to any decision it had to come from Hasler. That is the way it should be but it didn't make it any easier for me. I'm not kicking, I'm just explaining what my job was and how far I could go in any direction. No place.

So after studying the situation and consulting Fulton Lewis Jr., Hasler comes up with this bright idea. "Fire Williams!"

He figured that would solve everything.

*A Country Merchant, sometimes known as the Man behind the Face, was sitting in his Prunery one Day when a Drummer came in to sell him a lot of Goods he didn't need.*

— GEORGE ADE

# *16*

THE ATTEMPT on the part of Sleep Tite Top Management to fire Catherine Williams was one of the most colossal fizzles in the history of American industry. Also the shortest.

First I tore up the note in a fine frenzy and just sat cussing for about five minutes and raising hell with the universe.

"And Williams of all people," Mabel said. "Oh my god."

"Well, this is where the poor but honest young foreman goes into the big boss's office and tells him off," I said. "I don't have to take this kind of . . ."

"Oh my god," Mabel said. "Where are my Tums at? What a day!"

I combed my hair and took the elevator down to the main office and walked down through the office while the stenos stared at me and lost a couple of beats in their gum symphony and I walked right into Hasler's office. He was on the telephone so I backed out the door to wait, but not before I heard him saying:

". . . and every red-blooded believer in the free enterprise system should sit down and write Hickenlooper and tell him . . ."

I stood outside and the elevator boy went by and winked at me. First sign of life I ever saw out of him. I felt like a sap, standing there outside the principal's office, but it wasn't for long. Hasler hollered, "Come on in, Sorokin, come on in."

His office looked like the wealthy railroad president's office in one of the 1910 silent movies where the hero shoots his cuffs and rolls his eyeballs almost into the camera. It was all there, the black-oak trim, the black-oak chairs, the black-oak hatrack, the black-oak desk, the wire letter basket, the chromo of the Falls of the Yellowstone, the steel engraving of General U. S. Grant, the photo of the Board of Directors in high collars, and even a nickel-plated stand-up telephone.

"I got your note about Williams," I said.

"Naturally. Well what about it?" he said, arranging his jaw into "fighter" position. "Did you can her yet?"

"Look, Mr. Hasler," I said. "We're sitting on a keg of gunpowder up there. The help is sore about no wage increase so they started this slowdown to bring the thing to a head. If we fire Williams we'll play right into their hands. They'll . . ."

"Nonsense," he said. "The girl's a troublemaker. Probably all full of socialistic crazy ideas. She's . . ."

"They'll claim she was fired without cause and by tomorrow morning we'll have a strike. Not a machine will sew a stitch tomorrow. The shipping room will have to close down and somebody will have to . . ."

"No strike. I won't permit a strike on these premises. I . . ."

". . . and somebody will have to write *our customers and tell them they are not going to get their pajamas for the holiday trade*," I said. I was talking plainer than I ever had with Hasler, but I was through playing around — I figured if he gives me the air so much the better, let the silly bastard fire me and I'd go smell the breezes off Lake Michigan again.

"Never mind about the customers," he said. "Your job is the factory," he jabbed a finger at me.

"And then at the end of the year," I said — I was getting mighty hot and unattractively red in the face — "then at the end of the year somebody will have to explain to the stockholders how come we had a strike and lost half our holiday business and how come no dividends."

He slowly puffed up like an insulted toad at this — he

was so flabbergasted he couldn't say a word, he just stared at me — "balefully," what I mean.

"All right then," he said, finally, like somebody had stuck a pin in him and he was slowly deflating. "You're supposed to know labor relations." He had a mighty funny look on his face, like he was getting some sense for a welcome change.

One of the office girls came and stuck her head around the corner of the door. "Excuse me," she says in her usual flat voice, "but can you sign these checks now, Mr. Hasler? Mr. O'Hara is out and won't be back."

She gave him the checks and he signed them and all you could hear was the scratching of his old stub pen, and I gazed innocently out the window at the dirty sky that looked like the sun had gone on a sympathy strike with the Sleep Tite girls. Then I looked at General Grant and then at the girl and by god *she* winked at me. She was one of these fresh young squirts from the Business College that had been here just long enough to know I was new and a Big City Boy and that Hasler was some kind of a laff, so she winked. A winking girl is quite a novelty actually. I began to feel a little more confidence in my future in the garment trade.

"You claim they *want* us to discharge this Williams girl?" Hasler said when the winker had departed for the accounting dept. The idea seemed to surprise him. He looked puzzled, like a dribble-glass victim.

"Why sure they do, Mr. Hasler," I said, switching to a more informal, practically humble tone (after the way I'd been talking).

[     164     ]

"Maybe you're right," he said, swiveling around in his old slat-back chair with the shiny black leather seat.

"And Rubenstein is coming next week," I said. "We've got to face this thing sometime."

"No wage increase!" he shouted all of a sudden, and slammed his fist down among the untidy papers on the black-oak 1911 desk. "You don't have to fire Williams, maybe, but no increase! We're going to fight this thing, Sorokin!"

Let him find out for himself. Let him and Henry B. Walthall and Francis X. Bushman have a conference and plan a course of action to take against the Associated Garment Workers, Local 561.

"Rubenstein will be here Monday A.M.," I said.

"Rubenstein," he said. "A very tricky fellow. Very clever fellow that one."

"I got Murdock's note about collars," I said. "We'll check those patterns."

"Do you know Rubenstein, Sorokin?"

"Sure, I know him."

"What about him?"

"He's smart. That's all I know. And he can get tough, so I hear."

"Did you hear Fulton Lewis Jr. last night?" Hasler said. "It seems there's this bill to make Labor Unions unconstitutional and Fulton Lewis says . . ."

"My radio is busted," I said.

I went back up to the factory.

"Well everything is gonna be jake," I said, sitting down at my desk. "Everything is going to be fine."

[     165     ]

"Thank the lord for that anyways," Mabel said. "I ate three Tums since you went down to the office I was that worried. What happened?"

"Well it seems there is this bill in Congress, or maybe it isn't quite there yet, but anyway it is going to make Labor Unions unconstitutional. As soon as it becomes Law why we are going to can Williams and cut the minimum wage to 25 cents an hour. So you see everything is all O.K. and nothing to worry about. Hasler is not so dumb as he looks, see?"

"Well I am reliefed to see you in a joking mood again," she said. "But what happened?"

So I told her what happened, including the winking office girl, and she said she was glad I had made a good impression and not got mad at Mr. Hasler because she was getting use to having me around and a few jokes once in a while and all that and she would not like to of seen me get fired just yet.

"Here's your copy of the Sleep Tite *Flash*," she added. "Why don't you just set down and for once I'll close the door and you relax a little and read the *Flash* and relax."

She closed the door and set my mimeographed copy of the Sleep Tite *Flash* on the desk in front of me.

"By the way, what did he say about that Murdock letter and them terrible collars?" she said, working the slats on the Venetian blind too far one way, then too far the other way.

"I mentioned it but he said nothing. I believe he had forgotten all about it already," I said.

[    166    ]

"Do you want a piece of divinity fudge?" Mabel said. "It come from the Luthern Church social."

"O.K., give me some Lutheran fudge," I said.

"ARE YOU CASHING IN ON SPOT BUSINESS????" the Sleep Tite *Flash* said:

We are getting some swell immediate orders from some of you boys who are still out plugging the Spring Line. Here's some honeys that whizzed into our midst this week, *and were shipped out* (most of them) THE SAME DAY:

| | |
|---|---|
| Great Bend, Montana | $110 |
| Mt. Ayr, Iowa | 60 |
| Ft. Scott, Kan. | 170 |
| Casper, Wyoming | 50 |
| Napoleon, Ohio | 230 |
| (nice going, Ed Taylor!) | |
| Eugene, Oregon | 140 |
| Niles, Mich. | 195 |
| Newburyport, Mass. | 85 |

These little *additional* orders pay the same commission, boys, so get in there and DIG for the SPOT ORDER, when you are selling the beautiful Spring Line of Sleep Tite, the line of irresistible Sales Appeal for Men who *Care* at Bedtime!

JACK ROLAND does it AGAIN!

Gather round, gentlemen, and you shall hear a wondrous tale to our hearts so dear, a tale of selling skill, sagacity, and Sleep Tite Pluck and Determination. To wit and as follows:

Jack Roland speaking:

[     167     ]

"Ever since I took over this territory have been trying to land Marx and Klein, the biggest dept. store and biggest volume outlet in paj. in the whole territory. Of course we are a little high for them with our E–Z drawstring and other features and they have been featuring some eastern kike paj. out of Baltimore or Phily or some place and I could never get Mr. Jacobs the buyer even over to the sample room. He used for an excuse that he did not like our four-piece crotch construction. Anyway the store was very busy they are doing a nice fall business and store decorated very beautiful and really pulling in customers so I figured if I could never intice him to sample rm. in normal times I will never succeed now with the rush on. However when I entered the furnishings dept. Mr. Jacobs was very friendly and when I asked him to come over to sample rm. instead of giving me the brush off he says he can get away at 3 P.M. Upshot of it was I sold him a bill (enclosed) of over a $1000.00 for spring. This was all due to my going in the store whereas I was so discouraged over this acct. I almost never even went in to see Jacobs at all. The reason for it was he says he has changed his mind about our four-piece crotch and is going to give it a whirl."

*That's* what we call "sticking" until it hurts. And does it pay off!! Ask Jack Roland!

But to get away from the serious side of things for a moment . . .

"How about another piece of divinity?" Mabel said. "O.K.," I said.

. . . away from the serious side of things for a moment, we modern Sales Engineers with our scientific and

[    168    ]

streamline methods of selling may tend to look with a smile or perhaps even a sneer at the old-fashioned drummer with his hearty handclasp, but maybe we with all our technical knowledge are lacking something these old-timers had in abundance, namely a SENSE OF HUMOR!

Sometimes there are times in every salesman's career when a grin or a hearty laugh will win the day. Here's one we read someplace the other day which illustrates our point:

Take the case of a young salesman who had been trying for days to see a certain very hard-boiled executive. This executive was a tyrant, an old curmudgeon who even the old experienced salesmen found a vexatious problem.

Finally the young salesman gained admittance to "the Lions Den" and walked in, striving with all his might to look cool, composed, and forceful.

Just then the salesman stepped on a freshly waxed spot on the floor, both feet shot out, and he found himself sprawled on the floor. There was nothing in his sales manual to cover a situation like this, so he cast technique to the four winds and simply laughed. The executive was but a breath behind him. When their mirth subsided they visited, and out of this visit grew an order running into hundreds of dollars.

See What We Mean? How's *your* sense of humor? There's a lot of truth in that story if you just think it over, don't you agree?

"Say Mabel," I said. "How long is it since this floor was waxed?"

"Why only last week. What's the matter with it?"

"Oh nothing."

"Don't it look all right?"

"Yeah it looks O.K.," I said.

For your information we have booked the BIGGEST
PAJAMA BUSINESS in our history dating back to 1912. Our
factory is working at top speed to assure all loyal customers
and New Accounts that their gloriously-styled Sleep Tite
pajamas will be shipped promptly for the Holiday trade.
From the cutting room through the sewing floors and
down to inspection, each Sleep Tite employee is literally
"knocking themself out" to boost production and deliver
the goods *where* it's wanted, *when* it's wanted.

"Haha," I said. "Some humorist is evidently writing this
bulletin now."

"What's the matter?" Mabel said.

"Nothing," I said. "Give me another hunk of divine
fudge."

*Please send me the names of any insane customers who buy number 760 at $72.00 as I have some gold mine stock of my grandfathers which they would no doubt take off my hands in a minute. Anybody who would pay $72.00 doz. for that lousy number would give me a nice price I imagine. Have you all gone nuts in there?*

— FROM THE TERRITORY

# 17

THAT WAS FRIDAY and after work I went home in a mighty poor frame of mind. I flopped on my studio couch in my studio and smoked five cigarettes into my large glass ash tray weighing eleven pounds and the world seemed a tedious affair.

I picked up the phone and called Babe. While waiting

[      171      ]

for the connection I decided that the only thing in the world of any consequence was the fact of Babe, me, love, romance, passionate clasps and sighs, being together anywhere, under the neon glow of midnight in some ratty street where the late Midwestern wind of October blows the loose papers around in the gutter, or parked behind the Junior High School in an alley, or dancing, across the Mississippi, to accordion music, or just together anyplace. In a split second I felt better and the world seemed bright and gay.

"Hello wonderful," I said to Babe.

"Hello," she said.

"Where are we going tonight?" I said. Already I could smell the French fried potatoes, hear the accordion playing "Nola" or "Doll Dance," see Babe's green eyes across the table, feel her fusing into me on the dance floor.

"I guess you didn't understand what I said the other night," she said.

"I guess I didn't," I said. "What's the story, honey?"

"That's a swell new expression, that 'What's the story?' What is that, something new like 'Out of this world'?" she said.

"Now just what seems to be the trouble up there?" I said. "What happened, did you scorch the sauerkraut or something? Come on, sweetheart, don't be like that. What time shall I pick you up? It's Friday night and baby am I ready to take off in an aerial balloon. What a week!"

"Too bad about you," she said, very cold and far away.

"All right. What is it you told me the other night?"

"I told you until this thing is settled you and I are not going out together any more."

"But baby, you didn't mean that. Why you and I . . . Why listen, I simply got to see you tonight or go nuts. Baby . . ."

"Never mind the 'baby' stuff. I meant it. Anyway I got to go over to Wisconsin tonight with Dad to a wake. My uncle died."

"Goddamn it your uncle won't miss you and I will. Babe, I need you tonight," I said. "I want to talk to you. I have to sit and look at you. I'm in a bad way, darling."

"I have to go," she said.

"You mean you don't want to go out with me," I said.

"Take it that way if you want to, but I didn't say so."

"Well it sounds like it. Who is this uncle anyway?"

"Oh my god Sidney, don't be so damn difficult," she said. "It's my Uncle Frank — now you don't know any more than you did before."

"I know I love you, Babe," I said, in a pathetic voice. Maybe Gable could have done something with the line, but with me it just sounded goofy as hell.

"I've got to go," she said. "I've got Dad's supper on the stove."

"I said I love you, didn't you hear me?"

"Yes I heard you, what am I supposed to do, bust out crying?" she said.

"Babe, do you love me?" Boy, was I desperate for a crumb of affection. What a Friday night after a rough week.

"Yes," she said. "I'm delirious on the subject. Honest, I got to go. Call me Sunday, Sid."

"Do you really?" I said. "I'm crazy about you Babe. I love you, love you, love you, got that?"

"Say are you drunk?" she said. "Call me Sunday."

"Do you hear me?" I said.

"Yes, you dope," she said and hung up.

That was the beginning of a mighty big and overpowering night. Oh, you Babe, you should have gone out with me and kept your Own True out of trouble. But that's what happens. That's what happens when a woman gets the idea that she is being dramatic. As for the slowdown, she was only doing that out of a determination to stir up some new and unusual emotions, too. She didn't really give a goddamn about the 7½ cents like some of them did, but she sure enjoyed kicking up a fuss, irritating Hasler, getting a hand from the other girls, further complicating our love affair and getting more or less into the movie scenario field.

I went out to the kitchenette and poured myself a double Old Hickory and sat on a kitchen chair and listened to the weather report over the radio and talked out loud to Babe and it was quite a conversation. Then I called her again but it was even worse and she said she and her Dad were getting ready to go to Wisconsin to this wake and I would have to hang up because she was busy and I should call her Sunday.

I finished my drink and looked at the view of Niagara Falls on the kitchen calendar for a while and then changed my shirt and went out. I got halfway down the stairs

[    174    ]

and decided what I needed was another drink so I went back and poured out another one and sat there in my topcoat with my hat pushed back like some hot shot newspaper reporter in the movies. Then I figured well I can go through the motions, and just calling her number will make me feel a little better and no danger of being unhappier because Red won't answer anyway with her voice, because she's gone. So I did it and there was no answer. That made me feel better so I got another hunk of ice and made another highball. Then I walked out into the other room and I looked at "The Temptation of Indiana Harbor" and I said "Well Harry they have not pulled my teeth yet, kid, but you have to watch them awfully close," and I turned on the radio again and it was the Symphony Hour, from the State University and they were halfway through the *Pathétique*. I got a big lump in my throat and went in and sat on the bed and I said "I said I love you, kid, did you hear me?" And Babe said "Yes, you dope."

I lay down and talked to her for a while and fell asleep and when I woke up it was eight o'clock and I gave my face the cold water treatment and had a triple and went down to the Elks Club.

I was feeling like one thousand dollars by then and I went to the modernistic bar and the modernistic bartender gave me a highball and I talked to him about our different experiences on Guam and in Hawaii and all that. And then two boys from town sat down next to me, and about ten o'clock we were all loaded and arguing about what state had the best highway system and what year

[    175    ]

four-wheel brakes had come onto the automotive scene, and were demanding preference from the bartender in being allowed to pay for the drinks.

They were talking all the time about this party they were about to go to, and they said I had to come along too.

"No I'm not going to any party," I said about a million times. "Anyway, nobody invited me and I have not got to the point where I . . ."

"The hell you're not," they kept saying. "What are you, some kinda snob or other? The hell you're not going to the party."

Then we would have an argument surrounding who was to pay for another round.

About eleven o'clock we got out into the street and one of these boys wanted to sing "The Road to Mandalay" but we got into the other boy's car and drove all over hell and back again, up and down those bluffs and I was looking in all the cozy homes where the lamplight was glowing and thinking how happy all those guys were sitting there in the overstuffed armchairs reading *Reader's Digest* — all they had to do now was wind the kitchen clock and go to bed, whereas I was forced to proclaim my hot-blooded young manhood by attending some crummy small-town party with a lot of people I didn't know or want to know.

"My girl is at a wake," I said. "That redhead of mine is over in Wisconsin tonight at her uncle's wake. Now what would you do with a girl like that who goes to a wake on Friday night and leaves a man all alone?"

"I'll guarantee this party won't be a wake," says one of the boys, whose old man owned nineteen filling stations.

"She went to this goddamn wake," I said.

"Where is this wake, let's go get her," says the other, who was some big cheese or other up at the Watson Pump Works.

"Here we are," says the first one. "Let's go."

"I don't feel right about this," I said.

"Come on, Chicago," says Frank the filling-station king. "Nobody here will probly know whether any of us are here or not."

Well this is a great big house, the biggest house you ever saw outside of the Potter Palmer house and double entrance doors four inches thick with art glass panels in them.

The joint was really hot and it struck me very funny in the midst of all the Victorian furniture, statuary, and hand-painted oil paintings of windmills, cows, and sunsets, to see the younger set at play. Some old boy was whacking out "Twelfth Street Rag" on a mammoth Steinway grand in one room, and then wandering around into another room twice as big with two cut-glass chandeliers in it you would run into this other group hanging over a Mason & Hamlin grand singing "A Million Dollar Baby" while the crayon drawing of grandfather over the fireplace quivered with the sour harmony.

They had the bar set up on a swell old marble top table and for laffs somebody was playing one of the old Whiteman 24000 series Victors on a windup phonograph over behind a rubber plant. Damnedest place I ever saw.

Above all the chatter, screaming, lousy singing and

corners filled with argumentative drunks or irate wives I could hear Bix and His Cornet and I went over by the phonograph.

"Jesus," I said to some boy standing there, "listen to Him. Oh if I could play the cornet like That I'd give up everything. I'd sit and blow that horn all the time."

"Yeah, you said it," says jellybean #1. "What did you say?"

"Bix," I said. "Listen to Him."

"Father who?" he said.

Behind me there was a crash and a crunch of breaking furniture and I turned in time to see a large boy lying in a mess on the floor on top of one of grandfather's collapsed chairs.

"Somebody bring me a drink," he said.

Everybody screamed and the group at the piano began on "Sleepy Time Gal."

"They will take it all in taxes anyway," said a boy in a gray flannel suit having a serious talk with a boy in a d.b. sharkskin.

"The only thing he will eat is Corn Flakes," says one matron to another behind me by the fireplace.

"I had the same trouble with Roger," says the other one, "but now he's in first grade he will eat anything."

Bix was through and I turned the record off carefully and went over to get a drink. There was nobody tending bar so I made a bourbon and water. Old Forester. $6.70 a fifth.

"God damn it where's the Scotch?" says a guy standing there waving the empty bottle. "Freddie, what the hell kind of a poorly managed saloon is this anyway? What kind of a bum saloon is this?" He had his coat off and his tie crooked and was red in the face.

"Hey, Freddie," he said. "This is a hell of a note. What kind of a lousy saloon is this anyway? The Scotch is all gone."

"Now take it easy, junior," says a good-looking black-haired guy coming in from the other room. "Plenty more where that came from. Hold everything, kid." He went out with the empty.

"Yeah well I thought this was a first-class saloon. Pretty lousy service I call it."

The kids around the piano were going on "Darktown Strutters Ball" now, with only about a quarter of them acquainted with the words and one guy clowning it by singing real loud as hell. A sloppy-looking brunette and a guy with glasses on were engaged in a kiss marathon behind the piano. Somebody spilled a highball into the piano.

"Never mind, that's good for it," says a little guy with pop eyes who was hanging onto a girl with horn-rim scopes. "That's good for it."

The matrons over in the corner got up.

"Charlie is tight again," said one. "I can hear his voice clear in here. I better go in there, much good that'll do."

"Stan has had Stella Morison cornered in there for an hour telling her what a genius he is in the stock market. I suppose I better do something. You can imagine how much Stella is getting out of that."

They went out.

A tall man in a tuxedo came in, sat down in one of the big red plush armchairs they had abandoned, and in one minute and ten seconds was asleep with his head falling back crazily and his mouth open. Somebody had been writing comical sayings on his stiff shirt with a lipstick.

There was a crash from the other room and a lot of noise, hollering, and feeble girlish screams.

"Hey Freddie!" says a guy with his hair all mussed up coming into the room. "Freddie! Where the hell is Freddie."

"What's the matter now?" says Freddie coming in the other door with two bottles of Scotch. "What's all the goddamn noise about?"

"Listen Freddie, we got to get Charlie out of here. He just took a poke at Stan. He's off again. So come on, let's get him out. Margie is O.K. If we get him to the car she can drive. He's getting mean. Come on."

"Here's your Scotch, junior," Freddie said, setting the bottles on the marble-top table.

"Get yourself another drink," he said to me as he passed.

"Want some help?" I said.

"Well, maybe. Come on along."

I followed him in and there was this great big joker, drunk and ornery and all balled up.

"Come on, Charlie, time for beddy by," says Freddie.

"Come on Charlie. Margie wants to go home."

"The hell with Margie," he says. "Who the hell asked her opinion? Did anybody ask your opinion, Mrs. Bishop, may I ask?"

He took a big swing at the boys who were trying to

[ 180 ]

get him out; Freddie ducked and fell over a coffee table and I got the punch right smack in the face. It knocked me down and the blood started pouring — what a mess. Some girl was putting a wet towel on my face and they were saying

"Keep his head down."

"That cold towel should fix it."

"Put his feet up on a chair."

"Give him a pillow."

"I wonder is his nose broken."

"That's the only time in his career old Charlie ever landed a punch."

"Give the guy a drink."

"Keep his head down."

Meantime good old Charlie, who would be out all over town tomorrow kissing everybody's ass and trying to sell some real estate or something, was being ushered out onto the frozen lawn and using language unfit for human consumption.

Some brunette doll was bending over me giving me the wet towel treatment. She had bangs and a black dress and some pearls and she was laughing.

"I'm sorry," she said, "but you looked awfully funny. You looked so surprised."

"Some party," I said. "I thought Gentleman Jim Corbett was in retirement."

"Just keep your head down," she said. "How's your nose feel?"

"Just wonderful," I said. "How's yours?"

"You're cute," she said. "What's your name?"

"Fainting Phil Scott," I said.

"How's his nose?" everybody said, standing around and gazing down at me from a height of several hundred feet.

"It's nice to be popular, anyway," I said.

"I don't understand how Margie stands it," a girl said.

"Ask me, she's about through standing it," another said.

"Keep your head down, precious," says the brunette. "Sally, get me another cold towel."

"What did he say his name was, Scott?" says somebody.

"This is one of the nicest parties I've ever attended," I said. "Can I come again?"

"I think it's stopping," said the brunette.

"He's O.K."

"He quit bleeding."

"Give him a drink."

"If I was Margie I'd be on my way back to Peoria on the midnight train."

"Who is this Scott, anyway?"

"He's gonna be all right. He's O.K."

"That goddamn Charlie."

I sat up. Somebody gave me a drink. I needed it.

"I think good old Charlie busted my nose," I said.

"Hey Doc, look at Scott's nose. Scott claims it's busted."

"Here's another towel," Sally said.

A guy wearing rimless glasses leaned over and palpated my nose.

"Ouch," I said. "Go easy."

"It's not broken," he said. "But it's a wonder. You feel all right?"

"Wonderful," I said. "Where's the tennis court? Let's play a few sets."

"You'll be O.K.," he said. "Give him two aspirins," he said to the brunette.

"Hey Doc, come on back here. Give us some boogie-woogie!"

Doc went back and sat down at the piano stool and began to play. Everybody left me alone and drifted around. But the brunette with the bangs and the pearls stayed with me and I got up and we sat down on a couch and she said, "Now how do you feel?" and I said, "I feel O.K. considering the shape I am in," which is an old laugh from the South Side.

"Weren't you there the night Frank Landgraf fell off the roof?" says this one guy standing by a huge bay window.

"No, I heard about it plenty but I wasn't there that time," replies sallow friend looking like he was ready for the turkish bath. "I heard about it but I was in Fort Dodge that night on a convention."

"Oh hell it was funny as a crutch, old Frank got to drinking these here stingers about 10 A.M. and by middle afternoon why he got this idea he should climb . . ."

"I had to go to Fort Dodge that day to this florists' convention," says the other one flicking his cigarette into an enormous jardiniere with some Grecian scene on it which cost sixty dollars at the Columbian Exposition. "The old man insisted I go to this florists' convention."

"I thought you were there that time. It was funny as a crutch."

"No you're thinking of Westphals' party over on the island. I was in Fort Dodge the time Frank fell off the roof."

"I thought sure you were there."

"No, I was in Fort Dodge. The old man insisted I hadda go to Fort Dodge. I wasn't there."

"Here's your aspirins," the girl said to me.

"Anyway by 3 P.M. Frank was going strong so after he put on a couple skits and pulled off this wonderful act with one of the kiddies' scooters why he somehow got up on the roof. Anyway we didn't even know he was up there when all of a sudden . . ."

"Yeah, he fell off onto Joe Grasshorn's head. I wish I'd have been there. They said . . ."

"Onto Joe's head and then bounced into the kids' sandpile. Cut his head on a fire engine one of the kids had left there and . . ."

"I heard they had to take nine stitches."

The noise from the piano and musical section got unbearable.

"Some of your friends have a poor ear for a tune," I said. "Why do they have this big urge to sing, anyway?"

"How does your nose feel?" says the doll with bangs and I said, "There is a certain sameness to your conversation but I love you anyway because you have passed me the wet towel when I needed it most."

"Come on upstairs," says the doll, "and I will give you one of my brother's shirts. Yours is all covered with blood."

There were 900 steps upstairs and then we were in a room with furniture in it like Marshall Field and Co. and

[    184    ]

a big hunting print on the wall, and I knew right away what was going to happen, drunk and busted-nosed as I was, although I hadn't thought much about it until halfway up the long stairs with flowered carpet and brass carpet rods, so when the girl with bangs and pearls propped me against a mahogany dresser and began to kiss me I was not surprised but wondered why it had not occurred to me before, while I had been lying downstairs with her leaning over me.

"You're pretty," she said.

"Oh god," I said.

"You don't come from Here, do you," she said. I ran my hand down her back and felt the taut, wonderful silken band of her bra.

"No," I said. "I come from Napoleon, Ohio, a whistle stop on the way to Paradise."

She began to kiss me.

"I'm loaded, baby," I said.

"Wait till I lock the door," she said.

Frankly I gave a mighty poor performance. In the first place I was loaded and also I was bowled over by the suddenness of it and I was nervous anyway.

"You're a flop," she said. "What's the matter with you anyway?"

"I'm drunk," I said. "I don't know what's the matter."

"This is positively insulting," she said.

Well, there we were in bed. Not just a bed but a four-poster bed with a canopy around the top. I had never seen one outside the movies. That alone was almost enough.

"Where the hell are your folks, anyway?" I said. The

[ 185 ]

door was locked but I figured somebody was going to knock it down any minute and start target practice on the bed.

"They're in Palm Beach. For heaven's sake relax."

Mostly I guess it was that I felt I was out of my social class. Here I was, all of a sudden projected between the expensive sheets with the famous Celeste Watson, for it was none other, and I was a boy from Gary High School.

"I never did anything like this with an aristocrat," I said. That was a goofy thing to say but I said it. "You're an aristocrat. You've got me all balled up, baby."

"Well then pretend I'm a waitress."

"You don't smell, act, or sound like a waitress," I said.

"You're a funny boy," she said. "How's your nose, funny-boy?"

"My nose is all right," I said.

After a while things got better when I got used to the idea, but not much better. Then they got worse again.

"Oh I never heard of such a thing," she kept saying.

"Baby, there's a lot of things you never heard of," I said.

Downstairs one of the pianos was still going and the singing was much worse.

"I better get out of here," I said. "I'm not doing any good anyway." The room was slowly revolving around and around.

"You're not going anyplace, lover," she said.

The bums downstairs were murdering "Old Mill Stream" now. Some pale moonlight came through the tall windows and glinted on the perfume bottles on her dressing table.

I tried to focus on them. Celeste Watson was kissing me some more.

"My poor old nose is busted," I said, and the perfume bottles rose slowly up to the ceiling and back down again and I said "That's nice, darling, keep on kissing me and kissing me and kissing me and . . ." And I put my arms around her and hugged her tight against me and buried my head in her neck. "The question is," I said into the sweet smelling hair, "whether a man of my age could become a Hotel Executive without any previous training. Your hair smells like springtime in Comiskey Park."

"You're crazy," she said.

"Good night Miss Watson, little wife," I said, and I passed out.

Sometime during the night I woke up and there was a frenzied consummation. She was slim and fragile. I kept thinking "My what a Big Girl Babe is by comparison."

She fell asleep and I lay there looking up into the canopy top of the bed. The moonlight had moved around from the perfume bottles and it fell on Celeste Watson's panties where they lay on the pale blue carpet.

*Frank was rather taken aback at the way things had turned out.*

— THE MOVING PICTURE BOYS OUTDOOR EXHIBITION

# *18*

SOMETHING HAD GONE WRONG but I was too confused to even try to figure it out. Mostly I hated the horrible voices of the evening, and the ludicrous singing, but all of us in the Middle West talk in this horrible flat whine so what does it matter, we will none of us ever articulate like Maurice Evans so let us concentrate on something else.

[    188    ]

Whether Myron W. Hasler cared or did not care, and whether he wore a polka-dot bow tie or a silk foulard four-in-hand poorly knotted, whether Harry Kosciuszko would ever have a color page in *Time* and whether Babe Williams had a dead uncle in a blue serge suit, whether there are any atheists in foxholes or not and whether Louis Armstrong's trumpet was of solid gold, whether cigarettes would stunt your growth and whether it would snow soon in the state of Montana — these were some of the whethers I sampled like candy bars gluey with Spanish peanuts, lecithin, and artificial color and flavor.

You think I'm a sap, don't you, I said, and Babe replied I sure do and all the time Celeste Watson lay beside me, naked and warm and I memorized her body with my right hand as I lay there right in the middle of the Middle West.

Would that I could fall in love with her, I thought — and tell her a lot of wonderful things. But I get so nervous around these big time dolls even if they are much dumber than me. They are so different. One could kiss the palm of her hand or just sit and look at her for a very long time — and when she lets you hold her in your arms you feel as though you were in a moving picture. Nothing you have ever known before bears even the most remote relationship to this new and strange experience.

Beside me all the time Celeste Watson, legendary bad girl of the area, lay peacefully dreaming of Henry Fonda, Life as It Should Be, and her new alligator shoes from O'Connor-Goldberg that cost Daddy fifty-five dollars.

She has so goddamn much money, I thought, isn't it

wonderful. But she has to go to the bathroom like everybody else. Only maybe she doesn't — there's a thought. Harry Kosciuszko said none of the movie stars did and I believed him.

Over the P.A. system came the voice of Roger J. Davidson, Sales Manager of the mighty Sleep Tite octopus and in his high-pitched voice he is telling the boys how to do it, how to be a success in the men's furnishing game:

"I've seen some jim-dandy orders in my time but I don't believe I've ever opened a finer bunch of salesmen's envelopes than I did at exactly 9:05 this morning. The orders for Lovers-On-Parade actually staggered us in here at headquarters as well as the new broadcloth number with contrast piping and remember, with our four-piece crotch you have got a talking point that will really deliver the goods to the alert retailer with an up-to-date sales-minded viewpoint."

I suppose, said Babe, that you think you own me now, just because we Did It a few times.

That's no way for a refined sewing-machine girl to talk, I said.

"Price seems to bother some of you men but take it from us — price isn't any object when the dealer once feasts his eyes on the snappy styling, luxury fabrics, and all around eye appeal of the Sleep Tite Line. So we say SHOW the Line, *show it again and again*. Don't talk, don't sing, don't shout, just SHOW! And you'll see commissions going up, up, and UP!"

What kind of a price, said Hasler, did you get on fluorescent tubes? Did you check the water rate? What makes you think you know anything? Did you hear Fulton Lewis last night? If not, explain why you are a Communist, which incidentally I suspected all along. Do you realize I have been in the garment industry over forty years? If you are Jewish why don't you admit it?

"Willy Stein writes us about the new lines as follows: Spring Claussen, of Center City, remarked today when I entered the store that he had already bought but perhaps he could give me a few doz. After I opened up and he saw our patterns and styling he gave me the 18 doz. enclosed. His brother-in-law is out of the firm now and they have put in new fixtures up front."

Another thing it looks to me as though you are stuck on yourself Babe said. So was Napoleon I said.

Celeste rolled over in her sleep and her arm fell across my face and without turning my head I lay there with her wrist against my mouth. I have heard about all this kind of stuff, I thought, in those two-bit books you buy around in the drugstores, and here it has happened to me; and I reached over and felt her and she was real and I looked up at the ruffles around the top of the bed and they were real too.

I suppose the redhead will hear about this some way or other.

GARMENT EXEC IN SEX TRIANGLE. SEWING–MACHINE GIRL SWEETHEART HINTS NUDE PARTIES WITH PUMP HEIRESS.

" 'I shot him because I love him,' said the shapely auburn-haired Catherine 'Babe' Williams from her cell in County Jail last night. 'I shot *her* to teach her some manners,' she added. Her large blue eyes brimmed with tears as she murmured, 'God how I love that boy.'

"Sorokin is in a coma at Sacred Heart Hospital after having sixteen bullets removed from his head; doctors say he will recover.

"Celeste Watson, daughter of industrialist J. T. Watson, is at the Schallenberger Funeral Home where friends may call after 10 A.M. tomorrow."

Mr. Hines appeared, picked the Watson panties off the carpet and hung them neatly over the back of a chair. — Now there's nothing to be alarmed about, he said. With this stop watch I simply take down the times of the motion elements of your job. Please proceed at your normal rate of speed and pay no attention to me. — Are you using Standard Data on this study? I said. — I'm afraid I have no Standard Data worked up to cover this job, he said. — Hines, you are slipping, I said.

Celeste Watson, the Pump Heiress rolled over, patted me on the arm, murmured "Your poor nose" and fell asleep again. Such a nose complex the heiress had.

If my uncle hadn't died now this wouldn't have happened, Babe said. He's your uncle, why blame me? I said. The idea of doing such a thing with this Watson female, she said. Come on in, I said, the water's fine.

Then there you are sitting there looking at the unearthly people that appear in the dining car — all looking completely awful like exhibits of contemporary America appearing photographically in *Life* and *Look*. They are all ill at ease in their city clothes and waiting for the next Ice Age: the big glacier will come down and wipe out everything:

humble blackamoors, shrimp cocktails, consommé Madrilène, individual chicken pot pie, Swiss steak, Spanish omelet, hearts of lettuce (French, Roquefort, or Russian?), assorted hot rolls and corn sticks, green apple pie, C.B. & Q. vanilla ice cream with chocolate sauce (and a funny wafer) or Choice of Cheese and Ritz Crackers, coffee, Sanka, tea or milk, mints, finger bowls — and what a relief all that will be to be forced gradually south by the big ice front moving inexorably toward the Mark Twain Hotel in St. Louis, then on south farther and farther to Memphis, Helena, and on down to Storyville and the docks of New Orleans, until all of us Rotarians and members of the Book-of-the-Month Club get shoved right out into the Gulf of Mexico.

Meanwhile the silverware on the spotless linen tinkles together with a musical sound and you look out the window seeing such things as:

Ghastly frame building falling down
Sign saying SAHARA COAL
Sign saying EAT
Sign saying SCHLITZ
Sign saying ACME LOAN CO.
Sign saying SHORT ORDERS
Sign saying MERCHANTS HOTEL
Sign saying RIALTO
Sign saying PARIS GARTERS
Sign saying VOTE FOR O'HARA
Kid with dirty face playing in alley
Upstairs bedroom with unmade bed
Two men arguing beside a telephone pole.

And then there is small-town doll all dressed up, cattle buyer who has put on weight since he bought his suit, and an inevitable soldier looking in dismay at bill of fare. Beside you, next to the coffee pot and sugar bowl, blushes the dining-car rose against the back scenery of switchmen's shanties, slum districts and cold barren farmland.

Where do these roses come from, that blossom above the linen and tinkling silverware of the dining car so full of perfume and pot roast?

### CHEW MAIL POUCH

And do they bloom eternally on the graves of dining-car stewards, pushing through the snowdrifts in Terre Haute and Missoula?

On to Chicago, the city of broken window shades and smudgy back streets, where the trains roll in and out endlessly and a thousand roses bob in the dining-car windows. Dining-Car Rose I love you.

I kissed Celeste Watson's wrist as it lay against my mouth.

I'm a fighter, Hasler said. The hell you say, I replied. I won't stand for a Strike, he added, there'll be no Strike in this plant. He picked up the phone and said: Hickenlooper, how's that legislation coming along? J. T. Watson is behind this thing and his daughter is right here.

Now you're talking, I said. And tell him my nose is busted.

Tell him my nose. Tell him.

*Babe where the hell are you?*

Tell him.

[      194      ]

*No man is genuinely happy, married, who has
to drink worse whiskey than he used to drink
when he was single.*

— MENCKEN

# 19

SATURDAY WAS AWFUL. There in my luxurious
suite, standing on the table, was the empty glass I had
drunk from the night before, on my way to my unpre-
meditated bedroom date with Sex-Crazed Heiress and a
bent nose. I sat down on a kitchen chair and made a quick
inventory of my assets. They included a condition whereby

my eyes would not focus properly, a semi-broken nose, a humiliating memory of failure as North American Love Champ, and a horrible longing for Randolph Street.

Called up Catherine "Babe" Williams but no answer. So I sat there and thought about her for a while and wondered How is this going to go if I continue with my Master Plan for Success, how is she going to fit in with the various details such as dinner at the Pump Room with an assortment of presidents and vice-presidents of different large corporations. She talks good English and she's funny and she's beautiful in a refreshing new-mown hay and martini mixture. She's English and I'm Russian and that will be interesting, I thought, and she will be a big success in the Kosciuszko group of . . .

(I went to the bathroom and put two large flat disks of Alka-Seltzer into a glass of water and carried them back to the kitchenette and sat down and watched it fizz)

. . . in the Kosciuszko group of artists, intellectuals, and funny, lovable, insufferable, horribly boring or marvelous characters (depending on the extent of your neurosis) into whose peculiar midst we might, if Married (what a thought!) be frequently thrown.

I drank a bunch of coffee and tried to relate the events in Celeste Watson's bedroom to myself. I must be a lot prettier a boy than what I imagined, I thought, but then it isn't everybody that comes from Gary, Indiana.

Oh my, the way my head felt was a crime against nature.

So the phone rang and I knew it was Babe and my heart went pitty pat as I went into the empty front room and knocked over a chair and answered the phone.

"How's your nose?"

So, the nose girl again.

"My nose is O.K. but my head isn't," I said.

"Mine too."

Pause.

"Come on up to the house," she said. "We're going to have a party."

"What, at 11 A.M. on a Saturday?"

"Oh just milk punch and stuff, or gin and tomato juice or something. Come on."

"Thanks honey," I said, "but I'm a wreck."

"You can lie down and take a nap. Come on."

"I *can't*, damn it. I'm played out and I don't want any milk punch or gin and tomato juice or rye and orange pop or anything."

"You're dopey. Come on," she said.

"Not now, maybe later," I said.

"Are you mad?" she said. "Because of your nose or anything?"

"No I'm not mad. I'm half crazy I'm so tired but I'm not mad."

"Are you mad at me?"

"Hell no," I said. "I'm just beat to a frazzle that's all. I'm in bed as a matter of fact."

"Yummy," she said.

"I'll see you later kid. You're wonderful and everything's wonderful and I'm going to bed."

"I'll come down to your place."

"The hell you will," I said. "I'll see you later."

"I'll call you at four o'clock," she said. In the background

I could hear some fugitive from the Jazz Age shaking a cocktail shaker.

"Swell," I said. "Good-by baby."

"Sweet dreams, you nut," she said.

My Alka-Seltzer was all fizzed out so I made a new one. I was beginning to get a twitch over my right eye.

Oh Lord, I thought, and Rubenstein coming Monday and me in this shape. I called Babe the beautiful sewing-machine girl but there was no answer. Some wake. Probably stayed on for a Wisconsin funeral.

I knew I couldn't sleep so I went down to the factory and sat at my desk smoking cigarettes and studying the piece-rate charts so I would look bright on Monday until the figures began to dance and then I fell asleep with my head on the piece rates. When I woke up it was dark outside and I turned on the lights and it was five-thirty. I went home in the gloom and took a bath and had a double, sitting in the tub and reading the morning paper and my nerves quit jumping around and my stomach grew warm and lovely. I tried to remember the piece rates and the average earnings in the different sections and I tried to think of some good arguments against the increase in case I would be called upon (which was unlikely).

The telephone rang and I went out dripping and it was Babe with a far-away voice.

"Hello Sidney. I'm still over in Wisconsin."

"Darling, come home," I said.

"Can you hear me?"

"Sure I can hear you. Say something."

"Oh Sid, I have to stay over until tomorrow."

"Come on home," I said. "I'm going crazy."

"I can't," she said. "You sound funny. What's the matter?"

"A long story," I said.

"How was the party?" she said.

"What party?"

"Now Sidney, this is Babe."

"How did you know I went to a party? Sure, I went to a party. Damnedest party I ever went to. Got drunk, got my nose busted — some party. Who told you about any party? What is this anyway? Where are you, kid?"

"I'm in Wisconsin someplace. My cousin Lucille just came in and she said Jack Niebold saw you and Richard Cole at the Elks Club last night with another boy and they took you off to a party."

"Some wide-open spaces," I said. "Did your cousin tell you where the party was?"

"No but Lucille says Rita Kazmaier told her there was a big party up at Watson's last night. She said you could hear it for half a mile. Sidney, can you hear me?"

"I can hear you Babe darling. Please come home."

"Sid, were you at the Watson party last night?"

"That's where I was. Honey, baby if you love me come home tonight. I'm in an awful shape."

"You mean you got in a fight at the Watsons?"

"No I didn't get in *no* fight. Babe your voice sounds wonderful."

"Listen Sid, can you hear me? How could you get hit if

you weren't in a fight? What happened anyway? What did the Watsons say?"

"I was standing there and a guy hit me. He was drunk and swinging wild and he hit me and my nose feels fierce and I feel worse and I want you to come home right now. I don't care about your uncle or anything I'm lonesome and I'm likely to get drunk and go crazy tonight if you don't come home. And the Watsons didn't say anything except they put cold towels on my nose. Come on home. I'll come and get you."

"What Watsons put cold towels on your nose?"

"Oh that Watson girl. The one that was in the International that night."

There was a long pause and crackling on the rural line and then Babe said:

"You've got quite a memory haven't you?"

"I can't hear you baby," I said. "What did you say?"

"Skip it," she said.

"Tell me where in hell you are and I'll come over and get you. I'll leave right now," I said.

"Oh you go on up to the Watsons again and have some champagne," she said. "I'm up here on Railroad Avenue and I have to stay home tonight and stir the sauerkraut."

"Babe! Are you off your rocker? Cut out all that crap and tell me where you are," I said. "I love you. I'm lonesome. I'm going bats. For god's sake where in hell are you?" I said, but the line was dead and Babe was gone.

I wanted to pick up my fancy modern art eleven pound ash tray and throw it right through the plate-glass window but instead I went out to the kitchen and looked at the whiskey bottle for a while and it said Old Hickory on it. Andy Jackson, I thought, and his Internal Improvements. So I had a double internal improvement and shaved and went to the Elks Club slamming the clutch and brakes on the old car as I went and getting madder and madder at myself, Babe, Watson, Hasler, and my folks for ever making me at all.

As a result of getting punched in the nose at Watsons I was High Society now, it seemed, because three very big Rotarians bought me drinks at the bar and the President of the Tri-States Utilities had me sit at his table and talk to his girl friend. He had about one-fourth of his hair and she was about twenty-six and made up like one of the girls at the 606 Club and she kept saying, "I guess people think I'm terrible because I'm so frank but I can't help it, that's the way I am. When I think something why I just blurt it out. I believe in being frank, don't you?"

"That all depends," I said, and the utilities magnate whacked me on the back and said I was funny.

"That must of been some party at Watsons last night," he said, relighting his Antony and Cleopatra while the waitress took our glasses away to be refilled with casite.

"I think Celeste is sweet," said 606 Club, looking around the room.

"What does Celeste think of you I wonder," says Utilities.

"You're cernly in a charming mood I must say," she said.

"Don't take me wrong," says Utilities to me, "but it

must of been funny as hell when Charlie landed that punch."

"Yeah it was pretty funny," I said.

"You're down at Sleep Tite aren't you?" he said. "You're the production chief they tell me."

"Yeah I'm the production chief," I said.

"Louie, I want another shartroose," says the doll.

"O.K., O.K.," he says. "But listen," he says, "tell me young man, what about Hasler?"

"Hasler's O.K.," I said. "He's my boss."

"Don't get on that now," says the girl. "Louie for god's sake let's talk about something besides business for a change. Honey," she says, "I want another shartroose."

"You had enough," he says. "Well I'll tell you about Hasler — Hasler is a horse's ass."

"You're the frank type too, I see," I said.

"Wonderful refined conversation," says the girl. "Just like the movies."

They went away and I went up to the bar and I was quite a celebrity even with the bartender, who asked me all about how I got punched and what time it took place and he said, "Little did I think anything like that was going to happen when you left here last night," and he gave me a drink and refused my fifty-cent piece.

"I hear they got two grand pianos up there," he said. "And a billiard room."

"I wasn't there long enough to check the billiard room," I said. "Listen, Buzz, who is this Charlie who socked me, anyway?"

"Oh, he come in here from Peoria or over in there someplace and is suppose to be a big riot on account he gets so drunk all the time. He's up there with the high ups, nobody knows why. His only talent is busting up furniture and that. Sober he's a very disinteresting-type fellow they say."

"Gee I love this town," I said.

"How was Celeste Watson?" he said. "Was she there?"

"Yeah, I met her. She was around there someplace. She was O.K. Then there was some doctor there looked at my nose after this wonderful Charlie hit me."

"Doc Higbee," he said. "Bet he was playing the piano, wasn't he?"

"That's the guy."

"That must of been quite an affair," he said.

"You're right about that," I said.

I got out into the street and found my car and went up to Watsons' to see the two grand pianos.

Same scene as the night before.

"Glamour puss!" Celeste said, greeting me beside a dusty potted palm and kissing me interestingly. "Did you have a lovely nap?"

"How is your good old nose?" Freddie said, handing me a Scotch and fizz in an enormous twelve-ounce cut-glass highball glass that shone beautifully under the twin chandeliers.

"Freddie, that was quite an experience," I said.

"You're at Sleep Tite, aren't you?" he said. "Tell me why they don't change that corny name, will you. Sleep Tite. Gawd!"

"Oh that started back in 1912 when they made mostly flannelettes, kids' sleepers, ladies' gowns, and stuff. Now

[ 203 ]

the trade knows the name so we have to keep it, I guess. Crazy as hell isn't it?"

"Not as crazy as Myron W. Hasler, the sheik of Araby," Freddie said.

"What is this, Hasler Night?" I said. "What's everybody so down on Hasler on account of? Hasler is an O.K. guy in his way. You ought to get out of pumps and into the glorious garment trade if you want trouble," I said.

Good god, now I was sticking up for him. That shows you something. What?

"Hasler's O.K.," I said.

"So is hay fever once you get used to it," Celeste said.

"What day is this, anyway," I said. "I'm confused."

"This is tomorrow," Celeste said and Freddie went away. There was no community singing anyway, but instead some imitator of Eddie Duchin was gently stroking the keyboard on Cole Porter numbers, and Celeste, with her perfume and black shining hair and a two-hundred dollar cocktail dress on looked restful and lovely for a very plain girl.

"Who is Freddie?" I said and she held my hand and I inhaled perfume.

"Are you kidding?" she said. "He's my brother, the white hope of the Watson Pump empire."

"The hell he is," I said. "He doesn't look like you."

"He's wonderful," she said. "Have you got a brother?"

"My brother plays French horn in the Chicago Civic Orchestra. He's quite a brother too," I said. "His name is Ivan."

"What the hell are you doing working for the Sleep Tite pajama mill?" she said.

[    204    ]

"Making a living, baby," I said, and we walked out of the room and down the hall and I took her in my arms and kissed her and I thought Babe, damn you, why don't you come home and let them bury that uncle by themselves.

There was a riot in the other parlor and somebody with two lessons was trying to play boogie woogie so we didn't go in there, we went wandering through one room after another hand in hand saying nothing.

"You know what I like about you darling?" I said.

"I'd like to know," she said.

"You have two grand pianos," I said.

"Oh, you rat," she said.

"And you've been outside the city limits, too," I said. "You're quite a baby."

"You ought to get out of that pajama nonsense," she said.

"Tonight I feel like that, too," I said. "I'm lonesome for Harry. God I'd like to see that ugly old Twelfth-Street station. Celeste, a big town boy in a small town is all a big mistake."

"Who's Harry?" she said.

"He's a crazy artist at the Art Institute."

"I'm rich but I don't know any artists."

"You don't need to."

"Your shirt's got blood all over it," she said. "Come on upstairs and I'll give you one of my brother's."

"Celeste, for god's sake," I said.

Babe, this is all your fault. I should never have come up here tonight. Celeste bores me. Freddie bores me. The conversation bores the hell out of me. I want accordion music and my Babe with the green eyes, my freckled sewing-machine girl. The hell with the two grand pianos and the hell with this Watson queen.

There was no moonlight in the bedroom this time and afterwards we went across the river and all got stupid at the Club 66.

*George I woke up the other night and lay awake wondering how Nels was getting along. Did he sell "Nutters" at Miles City a good fall bill of mdse? After fifty years on the road I can't help still thinking of my customers.*

— A RETIRED SALESMAN

# 20

MONDAY, Rubenstein Day, dawned cold and disgusted.

"I heard something about you," says the waitress to the truck driver while I was coming back to life at breakfast via the boiling coffee route over at the Elite.

"What was that?" he says.

"Oh that'd be telling," she says.

"Who said it?"

"Wouldn't you like to know?"

"You never heard nothing about me."

"The heck I din't."

On my way through the shipping room at the plant I ran into Joe Hayworth. He was from the cost department, a very fast boy with figures and all posted on Straight Time Direct Labor, Variable Merchandising Overhead, and Occupancy Cost Allocated in Proportion to Floor Space.

"Well, this is the day the big bomb goes off," I said.

"Yeah," he said. "Glad I don't have to get into it."

"How's business?" I said.

"It's terrific. Don't you read the famous Sleep Tite *Flash?*"

"I thought maybe that was bull for the salesmen."

"Not this time. Hell, orders are just pouring in."

"Well, I suppose if we have to give the increase that'll end."

"Whadda ya mean?"

"Well, we'll have to raise prices, won't we? Seven and one half cents increase. That's quite a burden."

"Who says we have to raise prices?"

"Why man, Hasler talks about nothing else. He says we'll have to raise prices and we'll price ourselves right out of the market and into the bankruptcy courts."

"Sid, you wanna know something?"

"What?"

"We put the 7½ cent increase in the costs three months ago."

"But goddamn it, we didn't give any increase!"

"I'll see you in bankruptcy court, kid," he said, and he strolled over to talk to a stupid-looking blonde who was chasing an order.

I went up in the elevator and I thought this will be a three-ring circus, kid, but you have nothing to lose except the seat of your pants so why worry. I could just actually *hear* the slowdown out in the plant.

"My god you look awful," Mabel said when I came into the office.

"Mabel, quiet down," I said. "I have been to hell and back since Friday night. And don't talk too loud."

"Babe didn't show up this morning," she said. "I figured something was going on."

"Got nothing to do with Babe," I said, sitting down and looking at a piece of mail which said "Are You Climbing the Executive Ladder to Top Management?"

"Say," Mabel said, "there is something funny about this. Your nose looks, well, I don't know, something about it."

"I'm O.K.," I said.

"How was the party?" she said.

"Oh hell," I said.

"I was at a brush party with Josie Landgraf Sunday and she says one of the Watsons' maids told her you were at the Watsons' Friday night. See, I told you you would get up with them high-ups."

"I'm up with the high-ups all right," I said. "But what's this 'brush party'? Did you say you were at a 'brush party'? What is that?"

"Why that's where these here women that sell brushes on

commission they get somebody to give a party at their house — you know, cards and light refreshments — and whatever the brush lady sells to the guests why the one that give the party gets a commission or some present or other."

"I never heard of a brush party," I said. "That's the craziest thing I ever heard of."

"No crazier than a Watson party judging from what I hear," Mabel said.

"Well, nobody tried to sell me a brush up there," I said.

"I bet they didn't. Listen, do they really have two grand pianos?"

"Yeah. Two of them."

"Just imagine. I bet that's beautiful in there. What's it like?"

"Mabel I'll tell you about it some other time. Today Rubenstein comes."

I went over all my production charts, cost figures, piece rates — all of it. But Babe was still out of town and I was suffering and suddenly I didn't really care any more whether Hasler thought I was Karl Marx or not.

I got up and went to the window and looked down into the street below.

"Did you ever hear about the time Frank Landgraf fell off the roof?" I said.

Mabel was typing up a letter to Singer and she finished her line and said:

"Why Landgraf down in the finishing department is his wife. He's dead now. The drink killed him. She's been here four years."

"They say he was quite a card."

"He sure was until it killed him," she said. "But I can't get over it, most of our superintendents we had here before could scarcely get into the Kiwanis and now you are out with the Watsons already."

"Maybe I should ask for a raise," I said.

"Rubenstein should be here by noon," she said, resuming her typing. "Then we'll all get a raise."

"Hasler says no raise."

"Everybody else gave it over a month ago. He'll give it."

"There's got to be an end to it," I said. "One raise after another. That'll put us out of business and you and I'll be looking for jobs."

"Ah phooey," Mabel said.

Mr. Hines came in and flopped down in a chair and simulated exhaustion.

"Now what?" I said.

"I'm up against a stone wall out there," he said. "The operators are in a very unsympathetic mood. Some of our best girls are down to the minimum."

"Don't worry about it," I said. "Mabel, give Mr. Hines a Tums."

"No thanks," he said. "It so happens I have perfect digestion. I think you would find that if you made a practice of chewing every bite of food at least fourteen times. . . ."

"How was the Foremen's meeting Thursday?" I said.

"Great meeting," he said brightening up. "Cleverest speaker I ever heard. It was really comical the way he presented his talk. First thing, when he was introduced he was talking in such a hoarse raspy voice, almost a whisper, that we could hardly hear him. He apologized for a bad throat infection and went off into a terrible fit of coughing. Well, we all felt pretty sold. After all, the committee paid him a good fee to come here and talk. It was really embarrassing."

"He had a big nerve, I'd say, to take the money," Mabel said.

"Well, he was coughing and giving his talk only you could hardly hear a word, when all of a sudden right in the middle of a sentence he began to talk in a normal voice as clear as you please. It was really good."

"Sounds O.K.," I said.

"I don't see how he could get over a sore throat as fast as all that," says Mabel. "Not if it was as bad as you was saying."

"Why it was all just a joke, don't you see," says Mr. Hines. "He didn't have any more sore throat than I have."

"He didn't? What made him talk so funny then?" says Mabel. "And how about all that coughing?"

"Why, don't you get it?" says Mr. Hines looking through his rimless lenses and wrinkling his brow. "The speaker was just pretending he had . . ."

"Never mind," I said. "I'll explain it to her later sometime, when we have a half holiday."

"How about coming to the Junior Business Builders meeting tomorrow night with me?" he said. "We are all supposed to bring a guest. We have a very dynamic speaker scheduled. His topic is called 'Management with a Smile.' I bet you'd get a lot out of it."

"Thanks, Hines, I appreciate it, but with the negotiations and all I'm likely to be busy. Anyway I've got to go to a brush party if I can get off."

"A brush party? What's that?" he said. "Is that up at the Chamber?"

"No, up on 23rd Street," I said. "The speaker of the evening comes in with two broken legs and a fractured skull but after he has talked a little while he gets out of the wheel chair and does a soft-shoe routine."

"You are always kidding," he said. "But I wish I could persuade you to come."

"I have sat and looked at my last plate of chicken à la king," I said, "and sung my last chorus of 'Smiles' and 'Tipperary.' As far as inspirational meetings are concerned, you can consider me retired."

Then I looked up and there was Rubenstein in his camel's-hair coat and white silk scarf.

"Sidney," he said, "you look very much at home behind that great big desk. How are you boy?"

"Hello Jake," I said. "I am in very poor shape."

"Hello, Mrs. Ellis," he said to Mabel. "How's everything with you?"

"Here, give me your coat," Mabel said. "Leave me hang that up for you."

Jake was a neat, small, quiet polite boy out of the New Mode plant in South Bend and another night-school boy who knew more about labor relations, law, and cost accounting than the boys who thought them up. The Associated had spotted him when he was involved in the historic New Mode negotiation as a union chairman and he had been handling the tough cases in four states for several years now. He was dark, and small, and a little bit ugly, and you would never hire him to sweep out, if he came into the employment office in a pair of dirty pants, but there's where you would be making a mistake, which just goes to show. Now he had on a nice gray flannel and a ten dollar extra-fine pima cotton white shirt with a neat foulard tie and Jake looked very nice. He had quite a bit of nose but so have I so we won't bring that up. His was in a hell of a lot better shape than mine on this gray Monday morning.

I introduced him to Mr. Hines and Hines said, "I hear that Blum and Harris have put in those new electric thread clippers. How is it working out? Have you been in their plant lately?"

"They signed up three months ago. I haven't been there since," he said.

"What did they sign for?" I said. Mabel came over and laid a brand new virgin roll of Tums on my desk behind the calendar.

"Seven and a half cents," he said. "Don't you read the papers?"

"I'm a slow reader," I said. "Reading is an effort to me."

"Sid, this is curious to see you here. How do you like it?" Jake said.

"How many have signed for 7½ cents?" I said. "How many in this area have already signed?"

"Everybody," he said. "And everybody in the East too, except Lowenstein and they're going out of business so we let them alone."

"How come you let us alone so long?" I said.

"Can I smoke in here?" Jake said.

"Go ahead," I said. "Smoke your head off."

"How's Mr. Hasler?" he said.

"That covers a lot of ground," I said. "Mr. Hasler is all right."

"I bet you people put the increase into your costs last summer," Jake said.

"Don't be ridiculous," I said. "You're not going to get any increase here. We got distribution problems here. We can't compete with Fullbright and Rigney-Selwyn and Ace-High and those guys. You know that. Give us a break. Without a cost advantage on the rates we're out of business."

"Forstman Overall in Oskaloosa signed up," he said. "They're competing with Lee, Oshkosh, and all the rest of the overall people. Ben Franklin Glove and Mitten signed up. Sixty-five machines and competing with Wells-Lamont and the big boys in the work glove game. What are you talking about, Sid, you know better than that."

"Our men are meeting a lot of sales resistance this season," Mr. Hines said, clicking his stop watch.

"Pajamas isn't what it used to be," I said. "Nobody wears them any more. Brother it's tough."

"Yeah, I've got your sales figures. They look tough."

"That's the way it goes," I said. "You got our sales figures?"

"Sid you're getting fat, putting on a little weight aren't you?"

"Not this week I'm not," I said.

"I've got a date for a quiet little talk all alone downstairs with Mr. Hasler at 2 P.M.," he said.

The noon bell rang and the machines stopped, one by one, the hum and whirr stopped and we sat there listening. Hines and Mabel went down to the lunchroom to eat.

"You're still on line shafts here I see," Jake said. "Haven't you talked to Mr. Hasler about that?"

"You talk to him," I said. "You talk to him about that when you have this nice little meeting with him this afternoon."

"Sid you were always a smart boy. What did you get into this outfit for anyway?"

"Oh the hell with you, Jake," I said.

He shrugged his shoulders way up to his ears like Papa.

"Pardon me," he said.

Jake went out to eat and I went down and had a sandwich and coffee in the lunchroom, and a piece of gluey pie. Mabel had gone uptown and I sat there drinking coffee and looking wise, and the girls jabbered and ate out of paper bags and down at one end, some of them were playing cards. The old ones just sat and looked straight ahead, not talking, not doing anything, just waiting for the bell.

The slowdown was a dirty low trick, I thought; we would never have pulled such cheap mean stuff on Shapiro. I looked at the women and girls and I thought You stupid females, you lousy old bums, there is hardly an operator among you. You are lazy and whining all the time and your work is rotten — you are skip-stitching, leaving seams open, leaving raw edges, mixing colors, getting oil on garments, twisting fronts, ruining collars, spoiling buttonholes, breaking needles — you are a disgrace to a sewing room and yet you are hollering all the time for more money, you ignorant, busted-down bums. What you ought to get is a *cut,* not an increase. Haha! how would you like *that,* you wonderful old tramps, you. You are causing me more trouble than the World War.

Mabel came in all bundled up.

"Say, did it ever turn cold out!" she said.

"Where you been anyway?" I said.

"Up to the funeral parlor."

"Who's dead now?"

"Old Mrs. Schilsky. You wouldn't know her. You should of seen the flowers."

"I wish I could," I said. "Who's old Mrs. Schilsky?"

"Well, I never knew her but her son married a girl that used to live next door to us in Cuba City when I was in grade school."

"You mean you went out in the cold just to see some old girl dead that you never saw alive? What's the idea, are you getting silly?"

"I did too see her alive. I seen her one time on the Oxus Cauldron excursion boat ride to Cassville."

"How'd she look?"

"When? Now or on the boat ride?"

"Either time."

"Oh she was just a fat old thing. But I must say there was beautiful flowers."

"Think I better go up and have a look?"

"Oh you're the silliest man I ever met. Why should you go up there? *You* don't know her."

"Looks like I know her as well as you did," I said.

"I got to do something besides sit around here all noon hour. You never know where you'll meet somebody interesting."

"I wonder where in the hell Babe is," I said.

"The funeral is at 3 P.M.," she said. "I don't envy them pall bears on a day like this."

*We all have to guard against creating moral
positions out of temperamental desires.*

— LOUIS KRONENBERGER

# *21*

NOTHING MORE HAPPENED that day and the next
morning I got up wondering what in the hell had gone on.
You are in swell shape, Sid, I said to myself as I was
shaving. You have got yourself right in the middle of a
slowdown and an idiotic union-management hassle with
both sides sore at you, you have a swell girl that looks like

[ 219 ]

Rita Hayworth but you got drunk and laid some rich girl, got your nose busted and made a damn fool of yourself, you look all beat to hell and your brains have turned to Orange Jello.

So to make it a hit performance I managed to cut myself with the razor.

That must have been some wonderful meeting Rubenstein had with Mr. Hasler at 2 P.M. in the black-oak office with the nickel-plated telephone and the color photograph of Yellowstone Park. I wish I had been there to see Hasler sweat and strain but I wasn't.

Babe was still over in Wisconsin. She had got tangled up in a mess of relatives and stayed on, it seemed, to see Uncle Edgar under ground and the last frozen clod of earth tamped into place. She had called me up the night before and we had had an unsatisfactory conversation with most of the talking being done by me, and me saying all the wrong things. Anyway she was still alive.

I walked all through the plant with my coat and hat on, with a sour look on my face and the operators sneered and some giggled and there wasn't any production going out — no production — these bums were just fooling around. They have no tempo to start with in these small-town plants, they are not geared to the incentive idea. We only had half a dozen real operators (Babe was one) in the whole plant.

I went in the office and tore a leaf off the daily calendar and threw it in the wastebasket.

"I hope Hasler and Rubenstein are getting along O.K.," I said. "It's getting late. We've got to get 6000 dozen lousy old Sleep Tite pajamas out of this plant so the ladies of bedroom discrimination can give their boy friends Sleep Tite Christmas pajamas."

Mabel was reading the Des Moines *Register*.

"Here's this case where the teen-age boy from Sioux City strangled his girl friend on the way home from some football game," she said. She had on an extra fancy dress for the big Labor Negotiations like it was Christmas.

"Is your husband a man of bedroom discrimination, Mabel?" I said hanging up my coat and hat.

"How you talk," she said. "My you're getting fresh. Your girl friend is still not here."

"She's still over in Wisconsin," I said.

"Here's a good one," she said. "It says here 'Narcotic Problem Put up to Churches.' That's a swell solution of this narcotics trouble and probably bad news for the dope addicts, as look what a grand job the churches have done in outlawing whiskey drinking and lip rouge and so forth."

"Don't be cynical so early in the morning," I said. "Especially when you are all dressed up like Dotty Lamour."

"They can leave the narcotics squad take over the rummage sale and meanwhile the church groups can spend the afternoon cleaning up the dope racket," she said.

"What happened yesterday?" I said.

"How do I know?" she said. "Mr. Hasler hasn't taken me into his confidence so far on the ins and outs of things."

"I bet that was some meeting," I said.

"Here's some farmer in South Dakota burned up his house with six kids in it and stuck a shotgun in his mouth and blew his head off," she said.

"He was probably a superintendent in disguise," I said.
Rubenstein came in and sat down.

"What's going on?" I said.

"Sidney this is the screwiest thing I ever ran into," he said.

"Oh you tell that to all the superintendents I'll bet," I said.

"Sidney, Hasler says he's not going to give the increase."

"That's what I told you, damn it."

"Yes, but he seems to mean it."

"He's a fighter."

"I heard about that, too."

"What next?"

"What's the usual procedure?"

"He'll call out the army, navy, and marines if you do."

"No he won't."

"Jake," I said. "Could you fix me up with a cutting-foreman's job in some nice quiet small plant with about fifty machines someplace? Come to think of it, I'd settle for belt boy or checking the incoming piece goods."

"You're four months behind in your union dues," he said. "Besides, you're on the ladder to Top Management."

"What happens next?" I said.

Mabel had her pocket mirror out and was patting her new hair-do.

"Hasler is calling in Hoffman," he said. "Hoffman's coming in on the morning train."

"The hell he is," I said. "Say, this is getting as big as U. S. Steel. Hoffman!"

Hoffman was a labor-relations consultant from Chicago.

[    222    ]

He beat the union in the Piedmont strike in 1938 and had a big reputation and his picture in *Time* magazine every once in a while, chewing on a cigar and glaring at somebody.

"Who is this Hoffman?" Mabel said. "I never heard of him before."

"He gives advice for five hundred bucks a day," I said.

"I would be glad to give Mr. Hasler some advice for only half that much," she said.

Hasler called me down to his office and told me Hoffman was coming and that he would bring him up to my office at 2 P.M.

"Our friend Rubenstein may be smart," he said. "But Hoffman is just a little bit smarter. I told you we would lick this thing."

"I sure hope so," I said.

"You don't look so good," he said. "Do you take enough exercise?"

"I haven't been sleeping very well. I've had this thing on my mind."

"Forget it," he said. "This won't take Hoffman more than half an hour."

They came into my office right on the button at 2 o'clock, and Hasler introduced me to Hoffman. He looked just like his pictures, including the cigar. An expensive suit that hung on him all wrong, an expensive tie that looked like some kid had tied it for him, expensive shoes needing a shine, and a rough, raspy voice that hurt your ears.

Mabel beat it and I closed the door and we all sat down.

"All right, let's have it. What's the squawk?" he said. "This is between you and the local of the Associated Garment Makers, right? They're negotiating an industry-wide increase of 7½ cents an hour, that correct?"

"That's correct, except I don't care for your phrase 'industry-wide increase,'" Hasler said, "and we are not paying any increase. Our costs are driving us to the wall already. We're refusing any wage increase. That's final."

"O.K.," Hoffman said, blowing some cigar smoke around. "How many of your competitors have granted this increase?"

"Rubenstein — the union representative — says all of them."

"Is Rubenstein here? I know Rubenstein."

"Yes, he's here."

"Well, if Rubenstein says they all signed up I guess they must have."

"Maybe he's lying."

"My god man, haven't you called up any of your competitors to find out?"

"We don't meddle in our competitors' affairs."

"That," Hoffman said, "is a unique way of looking at it."

"What are you going to do for us?" Hasler said.

"Hasmer," Hoffman said, "I hate to tell you this, but I can't do a thing except advise you to pay the increase. This is your rush season, ain't it? Yeah. Well, you can't afford a strike, and that's just what you'll get if you futz around on this increase any longer."

"They can't push us around," Hasler said.

"They already are pushing you around. Sorokin, what's your output in dozens at normal production?"

"Three hundred dozen a day," I said.

"What was it yesterday?"

"One hundred eighty-five dozen."

"So they can't push you around? What the hell do you call that? I know these boys in the retail-furnishings game. Brother, if you don't deliver your holiday orders why your salesmen won't even get their telescopes open next time they make the rounds."

"Offer them four cents," Hasler said.

"Too late. This is industry-wide stuff. They got a pattern. It's all cut and dried. You're not big enough to bust it. They'll close the plant and your customers will holler and . . ."

"Offer them five cents."

"You wanna go outa business, is that it?" Hoffman snarled. "You wanna be a hero, hey?"

Hasler was white. He stuck his jaw out. "I'm a fighter," he said. "I'm . . ."

"So was Dempsey," says Hoffman. "But times changed and Tunney knocked him off. Listen Hasmer, you don't seem to get the idea. Sure, you got smaller volume so some of your cutting costs are higher than Rigney-Selwyn and Man Styles Incorporated and Ace-High Nightwear and the other big ones. But nowadays there's what they call an industry pattern. The big ones, the medium ones, the little ones, they all go along."

[    225    ]

"That's not right. That's . . ."

"I didn't say it was right. I said that's the way things are. You wanna stay in business and sell your pajamas on State Street you gotta work on it from the merchandising end. You waste all your time arguing with the union about two cents on sewing down pockets and pretty soon you'll find all your customers are out in the Dakotas. After a while you won't even find *them*."

"The southern plants don't give a raise every time the help come in the office and ask for it. They don't . . ."

"They don't have the *union,* man. You're in the Associated Garment Makers, one of the biggest unions in the country."

"They're getting too much power. They won't last long. I don't approve of unions. They're unconstitutional, anyway," Hasler said.

"So are false teeth. But I expect to have mine for a long time. And I'm a fighter, too. The union is like false teeth, Hasmer. Once you got 'em you *gotta* like 'em." Hoffman chewed on his cigar and pulled out a big rumpled white handkerchief with a monogram on it as big as a silver dollar. He blew his nose and calmed down.

"Listen Hasmer," he said, "I can't do you much good. You wanna have another Homestead strike here, with Pinkertons, and shotguns, and dynamite, go ahead. I'll go back to Chicago and just charge you for today."

Hasler was right, but Hoffman was righter. Delivering the garments and depositing those checks from the customers was the main thing. Spreading that goddamn Lovers-On-Parade number all over the country and giving the stockholders a dividend. Keeping Babe and the other girls on the machines.

Hasler stood and looked out the window where a snow flurry was whitening the sidewalks. Hoffman smoked his cigar and said nothing.

At times like this I am always thinking of something goofy, something that has nothing to do with the subject at hand and I was thinking of Babe the night she made the westerns and then I started thinking of the snow and how maybe it was snowing right that minute on the steel mills in Gary, and on the El tracks on Van Buren Street, and I thought how quiet and strange it is in Chicago when a snowstorm drops down over the city and the taxis and trucks slide along silent and queer and the train whistles are kind of hollow and muffled.

"Oh," I hummed mentally, "and in the evening when the sun goes down."

The P.A. system started up out in the plant, full blast: "Just be-cause you think you're so pur-ty."

"My god Sorokin, get that damnable thing turned off," Hasler said, holding his head like a silent movie actor registering anguish.

I went through the payroll office to the music machine.

"Turn it off, turn it off," I said to Bernice. She was a little roly poly brunette who helped out on the payroll and was in charge of playing some records every once in a while to fire the girls up and "increase the output." ("Music While You Work in the Clean Modern Sleep Tite Factory. Sit-Down Work in Clean Surroundings. Music for your Enjoyment in a Friendly Atmosphere. Meet your Girl Friends at Sleep Tite," was the way our help-wanted ads ran. "And a Free Baby annually for those girls who qualify," the machinist used to say.)

"What's the matter?" Bernice said. "I thought you liked that piece. All the girls just love that piece. We had three requests for it already today. I was just . . ."

"Turn it off, honey," I said. "And leave it off. The Big Brains are all in there thinking. They don't go for Yankoviç, and they don't want Pistol Packin Mama or Dorsey's trombone, either."

"Oh gawd," she said.

"That ain't half of it," I said.

Mr. Hines was checking some time sheets.

"How's it going?" he said as I passed back through the payroll office.

"Just like you think it's going," I said.

"You know how many bundles Marie Baumgartner put out yesterday?" he said. "She's supposed to get out six. Yesterday she put out just three and a half."

"Well," I said, "maybe we'll get it straightened out soon. I hope so."

"That's bad. Slowdown like this can have serious lasting effects on the incentive."

I went back into the office and shut the door. Cigar smoke again, and Hasler staring out at the snow.

I don't know whether to laugh or cry over these things. Hoffman smoking his cigar, Hasler the great in the rumpled mud-brown job with black shoes; Hasler looking out into the dismal street at the snow and thinking how he couldn't hold up his head during the Fulton Lewis pro-

gram any more if he gave in to the union, Hoffman studying his wet cigar end and calculating his fee.


"Yeah, you and your big pal Hasler," Babe had said to
me. "I don't know why I like you when you have such
friends."

"My beautiful profile maybe," I told her.

"Oh Sid, don't you see, you shouldn't be mixed up with
a man like that. After a few years you'll turn into a Hasler
yourself."

"Maybe I should work up an imitation of Eddie Cantor
and go on the Broadway stage," I said. "Baby, I've spent ten
years in the garment trade and I know a lot more about it
than anybody thinks, even me. One of these days your boy
friend with the beautiful profile is going to Chicago and
walk into the office of Rigney-Selwyn and right into Sam
Selwyn's office. Sam Selwyn is gonna hire me for sixty-
five hundred and in fifteen years I'm gonna have his job
and play golf on Wednesday afternoons at the South Shore
Country Club."

"So. You've got it all figured out."

"Sure I've got it all figured out. I figured it out ten years
ago. And I'm not only on schedule, I'm about two years
ahead on my timetable. My patent plan didn't call for me
to take a superintendent's job for two years yet."

"You're stuck on yourself."

"Listen redhead," I said, getting kinda hot. "You think
all I know about the rag business is sitting on my ass in
that office talking to the Singer salesman and breaking up
hair-pulling parties between the operators. Well I've got

news for you, honey. I can draft and grade patterns. I'm a designer. I've worked in stock picking orders and taking inventory. I've worked in the shipping department. I know purchasing, cost control, inventory control, quality control, ulcer control and every other kind of control. I can make markers, run the elevator, drive the company truck and tear down and put together pretty near any standard machine. I know labor relations, personnel relations, public relations, and even a little about social relations. I've worked in men's pants, sportswear, pajamas, men's cut and sewn shorts, kids' rompers and playsuits, and work shirts. I've helped get up lines and I've worked with salesmen selling the line. I know finishing, ass-backwards. I know thread, buttons, zippers, needles, bias binding, buckles, kasha, broadcloth, rayon, wool, linings, silk, crepe, prints, wovens, machinery, equipment, light bulbs, sweeping compound and carbon paper. And what I don't know about any of this stuff I can bluff my way through on better than most of the sorry birds in his industry."

"My, my," she said. "Why don't you just step up to Hasler or Mr. O'Hara and admit right out that you're a genius. Maybe they'll make you president right now, or would that upset your timetable too much?"

"Let's you and me indulge in a little more love and a lot less hollering at each other," I said.

"O.K., genius, get to work," she said.

"And for god's sake let's lay off talking about this poor man Hasler," I said.

*　*　*

[　230　]

So there stood Hasler, looking out into the snow falling straight down softly in the late afternoon onto the dirty sidewalks of the industrial district, and thinking his own sad thoughts of defeat, humiliation, and disgrace at the Rotary Club.

"A nasty problem," he said, turning from the window as I closed the door behind me and sat down.

"You're making it a problem," Hoffman said. "But if you'd get over the idea of saving the entire garment industry from the bloodthirsty unions, which is like trying to push the Stevens Hotel down with a Model A Ford, and concentrate on increasing production and lowering your costs of manufacture like your competitors are doing, you'd be making some progress."

"And if I don't. If I decide to fight it out?"

"Then you'll end up making a fool of yourself and losing the company a lot of money."

"You don't mince words much."

"You're paying me five hundred bucks a day for my professional advice, not for a lot of poetry."

"Sorokin, what do you think of all this?" Hasler said. He looked tired and old and unhappy. "You're on the Management Team now. What do you say?"

"It's not for me to say," I said. "It's up to . . ."

"Don't play dumb with an old buck like me, boy. I hired you for your brains, if any. Now use 'em. What about it?"

"I believe they'll strike," I said. "If they strike we'll never deliver our orders. We're way behind already with this slowdown."

"You reel that off as though you had it all memorized,"

he said. There's the old Hasler again. For a minute I thought he'd lost his touch.

"That's what I believe, just the same," I said. "Times have changed. I don't like it any better than you do, but we've got to get our production back up again, and soon, and ship these holiday orders out. The factory is jammed with stuff in process and the shipping department is wearing out the telephones crying for stock."

"You said a million-dollar mouthful, young man," Hoffman said.

"Roosevelt. That damned contemptible cur," Hasler said. "Him and his unions."

*"You bother the hell out of me, too. That's
what they call love, baby."*

— MERLE

# 22

Hoffman went back to Chicago on the evening train.

"There is more to all this than reading Pegler's column
and squawking about the union," he said, as he got up
to leave. "You have an investment to protect here first of
all. Your stockholders want dividends. A strike will kill

[ 233 ]

the dividend for this year and you'll end up paying the increase anyway. They've got you over a barrel."

"That's all you've got to say for five hundred dollars?" Hasler said.

"Five hundred dollars *plus* transportation," he said. "Hasmer," he said, "why didn't you call me up on the telephone and describe the deal to me? You're trying to build this thing up into some affair of interplanetary significance. Let's face it, you can't buck this thing without running a very strong risk of going out of business."

"I don't look at it that way," Hasler said.

"I've got to catch that train," Hoffman said. He shuffled into an old beat-up vicuna overcoat that had cost three hundred dollars once upon a time, slapped a soiled Wendell Willkie brown felt hat on his head, shook hands, said good-by, and was gone.

Hasler sat there and you could hear a paper clip drop. I looked out at the gray sky and wondered what Errol Flynn was doing on his yacht.

"Well," he said finally, wheeling around and helping me inspect the expanse of dirty sky, "there's a good example of the type of wishy-washy thinking we have today. Frankly Sorokin, the man struck me as a Communist."

I thought, Time to move on, Sidney. Brother, you picked a real lemon here in the Garden of Love and you better get going before you are deported as an alien opium smuggler.

"I think Senator Hickenlooper would be interested in this little matter," he said. "I think Senator Hickenlooper is going to get a full report on the famous Mr. Hoffman with his picture in *Time* magazine. When we get through with him he might need that five hundred dollars more than he thinks."

I didn't say anything and Hasler picked up a paper knife and played with it and looked at me.

"Sorokin," he said, "what did you think of Hoffman's brilliant analysis of our labor problems?"

Oh, I thought, what the hell, Watsons have two pianos and Babe is still over in America's Dairyland and the cops are blowing their two-tone whistles on State Street and pretty soon Marshall Field's will put in their Christmas windows; Harry is painting a new picture and Stan Marco is pulling his Noel Coward routine in some nitery in Milwaukee, and the music goes round and round so I said, "I haven't got any stock but I'm supposed to produce the pajamas. I figure Hoffman is right."

"Sorokin," Hasler said, "ever since you came here I've been . . ."

The door opened and in came Mr. O'Hara, small and neat and tidy with his white hair brushed up in a pompadour and a yellow foulard tie blazing against a lavender shirt. He closed the door behind him.

"Sorokin," he said, "look at this." He handed me a telegram.

CLEVELAND OHIO 2 PM

SLEEP TITE INC. JUNCTION CITY IOWA

MUST HAVE COMPLETE SHIPMENT ALL ORDERS AS BOOKED OR CANCEL STOP ADVISE IMMEDIATELY IF YOU EXPECT TO DELIVER OR CANCEL REPEAT CANCEL

EISENDRATH STORES INC.

[    235    ]

"The Eisendrath account includes their whole chain of forty stores all over Ohio, Michigan, and Indiana," Mr. O'Hara said. "About fifty thousand dollars. Are they going to get their goods?"

"No," I said. "We've been down to nothing with this slowdown, and now it looks like a strike."

"Myron," he said, turning to Hasler who was an interesting shade of green. "I just met Mr. Hoffman on his way out and had a little talk with him."

"He's in cahoots with the union," Hasler said. "They got to him somehow and paid him off. He's as crazy as a loon. Communist, too."

"Myron," Mr. O'Hara said, "pay the increase retroactive to October first. Call Mr. Rubenstein in here at once and sign a contract."

"Sorokin," he said, "get out there into the plant and start getting those pajamas coming down the chutes. Put the girls on overtime. I want to see so many pajamas around here that we'll all have to take off our coats and pick orders. Get the idea?"

"Yes, sir," I said. "I've got it."

"Myron," he said, "When are you going to grow up?"

"I've fought this thing and I'll keep on fighting," Hasler said. "The whole thing is illegal and unconstitutional. They can't get away with it."

"Maybe you better go into politics, Myron, and straighten the country out," Mr. O'Hara said. "Come on down to my office and we'll discuss that possibility."

I was standing there with the telegram in my hand and Mr. O'Hara took the telegram and folded it up.

"Get going, Sorokin," he said. "Plenty of oil in the machines, and a bonus for the machinist. Orchids for the foreladies or whatever they want. Extra help, overtime, free coffee — but dump those pajamas."

"Yes, sir," I said.

"And Sorokin," he said, "remember, we're a quality house. Don't send any junk down."

"We'll double-check the inspectors," I said.

"That's the idea," he said. "Come on down to my office Myron."

I went through the payroll office and got on the P.A. system and Mabel came in while I was turning it on and she said, "What's going on? What happened?" and I said, "Baby just listen."

"Attention please," I said into the mike and I could hear my voice booming out in the plant very hollow and strange as the machines stopped one by one so the operators could hear. "Attention please. The management of Sleep Tite has just granted a 7½ cent wage increase to all workers in this plant. This increase is retroactive to October first. Effective the minute I stop talking to you the management will expect every operator in this plant to resume full production immediately. The entire force will go on overtime starting today. Our customers are waiting for their orders. Your jobs and your future depend on full production from every member of the production force. Will all foreladies and foremen and the machinist please report to my office at once. Now girls, let's get going and burn up those machines."

"Overtime!" Mabel said as I turned off the mike. "My

god that Hoffman sure must of made a five-hundred-dollar speech."

"Mabel," I said, "where has Mr. O'Hara been all this time?"

"Off hunting up near Canada someplace," she said. "I hear he killed a moose or something."

"He's not doing so bad here either," I said. "He just knocked over a two-hundred-pound Rotarian."

I gave the foreladies a big pep talk and told the machinist to sleep with those machines and I told Mr. Hines to put the stop watch away for the time being and just cruise the plant and help get the stuff out and I told the elevator boy to dump the comic books and look like he was alive and then I walked all through the plant and spread that good old infectious enthusiasm and fighting spirit.

I went back to the office and sat down and started to figure what was in process and what we could expect to get out and when and I was so excited I had to bum two Tums off of Mabel although one is my usual quota.

"One of the buttonhole machines is about ready to fly apart," said the Machinist coming into the office. "I been watching it for quite a while. It's getting bad."

"Call Singer on the phone and order out all the parts you need," I said. "Special delivery. Better double the order."

"Wasn't you a pall bear at Mrs. Schilsky's funeral?" Mabel said.

"Let him phone, Mabel," I said, "and we'll get the dope on the Schilsky rites later."

"Yeah," he says. "She was my mother's sister-in-law. They had one of these two-ton metallic caskets the dangedest heaviest thing you ever seen. Then they was three of us to each side and you can't take a long enough step; I kept tromping on old Roy Meyers's heels all the time. And that dang funeral director he come along behind, he could of grabbed ahold of the rear handle and lifted a little but instead he just lays his hands on top of the casket like he was steering it. He was a big help he was."

"Go on, Verne, call Singer," I said.

"Them expensive caskets is swell to look at but hell on the pall bears," he said.

"Get on the phone," I said. "The number is Calumet 2-0897. Tell them to get those parts in today's mail."

Then I looked up and Hasler was standing there and I thought, I hope Babe will go with me, I don't want to leave town with nothing to show for my trouble except a headache and an assortment of funeral anecdotes.

"Mabel, will you leave us alone for a few minutes, please," he said, and she went out and shut the door.

"Sorokin," he said, "we were in a bad way for a superintendent when we hired you. I had a hunch from the beginning that I was making a mistake but I decided to give you a chance. Your attitude . . ."

"I quit," I said. "Never mind the rest of it."

"Now, now, don't be hasty," he said. "You've been . . ."

"The hell with it," I said. "Take the whole plant and shove it."

"You've got quite a temper," he said. "You misunderstand what I came to talk about."

"I don't misunderstand a goddamn thing," I said. "You came up here to give *me* an ass-eatin because Mr. O'Hara gave *you* an ass-eatin. Well, that don't go with Sorokin. And you can tell that to your buddy Fulton Lewis too. I don't want to talk about it. I quit. You run the goddamn plant yourself."

I walked out on him and left him there talking to himself.

"Go on in and talk to Hasler," I said to Mabel, who was out in the payroll department. "He's lonesome."

"You look awful mad," she said. "Did you and him have a fight?"

"No such thing," I said. "He offered me a big raise but I've got a better offer so I quit."

"You *quit!* Oh my god," she said. "Where you going now? You don't mean to stand there and tell me you actually quit?"

"I've got me a bellhop's job at the Palmer House," I said. "I can retire in three years just on the tips alone."

When Hasler had gone away I called Babe's house but no answer. I began to think she had won some Wisconsin beauty contest and gone to Hollywood for a screen test. We worked the girls overtime until five-thirty and then I cleaned out my desk drawers and put my personal stuff in a Sleep Tite pajama box.

"He wasn't going to fire you," Mabel said. "You was crazy to quit."

"Not today he wasn't. But in about a month, after we got the orders out, he had me scheduled for the ax just as sure as you're born, honey. So I just fixed his wagon."

"He might make it hard for you to get a job. You leaving them in a spot and all that."

"Shapiro always needs a good marker and pattern-maker," I said. "Shapiro never heard of Sleep Tite. He sleeps in his underwear."

"That's all right for you," Mabel says, "but think about me. Now they'll hire some superntendent with a high collar and I'll have nobody to talk to again."

"I'll see if Shapiro has a spot for you," I said. "Then your old man can go to Wrigley Field and watch the Cubs fighting for cellar position every afternoon."

"I hate to see you go," she said.

"I'll see you tomorrow," I said.

I stopped at the Elks on the way home and had a much-needed double at the bar and talked about the wholesale crockery game with a salesman in a loud suit. I began to feel that I had made a fool of myself so I had another double and changed my mind.

"Competition is getting tougher every day," said my friend, who was drinking a bottle of Grain Belt.

"Did you make that line up or hear it someplace?" I said.

I went out into the street. A cold damp wind was blowing up from the river. I figured I would go back to my joint, change shirt, and go out and start hunting for Babe. I decided I would play like detective and hunt that girl up if it took me a week. Well, I had no job now, nothing to do, so I could spend forever combing over the whole state of Wisconsin if I had to. I walked up the street toward my place. It was raw as hell and people passed me in the early evening light of the swinging street lamps, carrying paper packages, milk bottles, newspapers — a sorry lot.

This was Tuesday evening and I hadn't seen Babe since Friday noon. This burying the uncle stuff was all for the birds. She just cleared out, that's all. Cleared out. Left me walking around the streets in the dark all by myself. Matter of fact if it wouldn't have been for her hiding out someplace, acting so goddamn female and leaving me all alone so I would get my nose busted and all, why everything would have been different. You might say it was all her fault anyway, wasn't she the cute little thing with her slowdown and all her bright ideas about strikes and lockouts and wages and management — small-town hick, she don't know any more about that stuff than Sister Sue. Nothing like one of these rubes with a lot of big ideas. So I figured the hell with her and I gave up this big idea to hunt her up wherever she was. I decided to hell with her.

Some drunk had finished off a pint and dropped the bottle by the sidewalk and I gave it a kick and it sailed through the air, bounced off a telephone pole, and hit the street with a musical crash. I walked on into the damp and the gloom and smelled the grease of different suppers oozing out of the three-story brick apartment houses with dim lights burning in the hallways.

When I got to my house I could see Mr. Beebe behind the lace curtains on the first floor, reading the evening paper in his three-way automatic, roomy luxurious, relaxing, open-arm Rocker-Recliner with Foam Rubber seat

[    242    ]

and Plastic Upholstery in Your Choice of three gleaming Modern Colors. I envied him, too. All Beebe had to do was read the evening paper, including three pages of obituaries, eat some fried ham sausage and German-fried potatoes and go to bed, whereas I had to go through a million motions and spend the next twenty years demonstrating my manhood to an uninterested world. Beebe was all past that, the bastard — his only problem was Getting Up Nights.

I went into the lower hall and smelled Beebe's ham sausage and picked my paper up off the staircase, unrolled it out of the tight, professional roll the paper boy had made of it, and stood there looking at the front page under the inadequate 40 watt bulb:

> *Teen Ager Stabs Father*
> *Teen Ager Admits Dope Ring Plot*
> *Teen Ager in Assault Denial*
> *Teen-Age Sex Orgies Revealed*
> *Teen Ager Admits*
> *Teen Ager Confesses*
> *Teen Ager Seized*

"Hell, I am in the wrong age group," I thought.

So I plodded up the stairs and stuck the key in the lock and walked in with the paper under my arm, ready to die at the thought of my empty joint and an evening alone with the radio telling me about Love, Fame, and the right cigarette to smoke.

And then there was the redhead, lying on my couch with two pillows behind her head reading *Life* magazine.

[    243    ]

I went over and knelt down beside this beautiful hick with the green eyes and I kissed her.

"Take your hat off," she said.

"I love you, kid," I said. "Did you get that wonderful uncle buried?" and I kissed her.

"Darling, you look tired and awful," she said.

"I'm all done at the plant," I said. "I told them to shove it," and I kissed her some more.

"I know it," she said. "I called Mabel at four o'clock," and she kissed me.

"You look so wonderful darling," I said. "I've had an awful time since you went away," and I kissed her neck and she smelled so good and I said, "Oh Babe, darling. Babe, Babe, Babe. You're my Babe forever."

"That's a long time," she said. "But I'll take a chance," and she kissed me. About every ten years you get a kiss that makes you feel as though you were spinning through space and this was one of those.

After that everything was beautiful, and then a couple days later I went back to the shores of Lake Michigan and I took Babe Williams along with me.

We were sitting in the dining car and the sun was pouring in over the tinkling silverware and snowy cloth; Iowa was getting farther and farther away and Lake Michigan getting nearer every minute. By the window the dining car rose bobbed gently with the motion of the train, and out in all the barren fields and farms the cattle stood around doing nothing. They were going noplace and would never see the Outer Drive at night or hear the els clattering down Wabash Avenue on a snowy afternoon. I wondered if the

Christmas decorations had been struck up yet on the lamp-posts all up and down State Street.

"Where are we going on our honeymoon?" says my beauty.

"Through the steel mills in Gary, Indiana," I said.